PHANTOM

OF FIRE

A DYLAN MAPLES ADVENTURE

PHANTOM of FIRE

SHANE PEACOCK

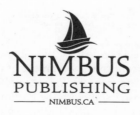

NIMBUS
PUBLISHING
— NIMBUS.CA —

Nimbus Publishing Limited
3660 Strawberry Hill Street, Halifax, NS, B3K 5A9
(902) 455-4286 nimbus.ca

Printed and bound in Canada
NB1387

Cover design: Cyanotype Books
Interior design: Heather Bryan
Editor: Tom Ryan

This story is a work of fiction. Names, characters, incidents, and places, including organizations and institutions, either are the product of the author's imagination or are used fictitiously.

Library and Archives Canada Cataloguing in Publication

Title: Phantom of fire / Shane Peacock.
Names: Peacock, Shane, author.
Description: "A Dylan Maples adventure".
Identifiers: Canadiana (print) 20189068841 | Canadiana (ebook) 2018906885X | ISBN 9781771087346 (softcover) | ISBN 9781771087605 (HTML)
Classification: LCC PS8581.E234 P43 2019 | DDC jC813/.6—dc23

Nimbus Publishing acknowledges the financial support for its publishing activities from the Government of Canada, the Canada Council for the Arts, and from the Province of Nova Scotia. We are pleased to work in partnership with the Province of Nova Scotia to develop and promote our creative industries for the benefit of all Nova Scotians.

For the Nan family:
welcome home, to Canada.

"Vision is the art of seeing what is invisible."

Jonathan Swift

Finn: *We'll use the Force.*

Han Solo: *That is NOT how the Force works!*

Star Wars: The Force Awakens

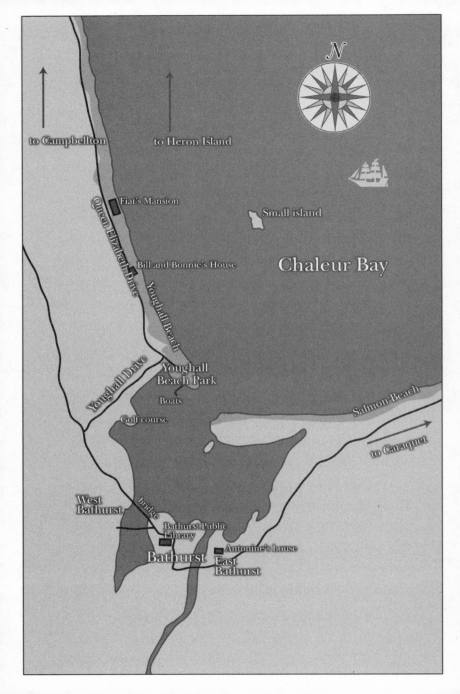

TABLE OF CONTENTS

1

NOT AGAIN

Toronto, Moore Park, somewhere north of middle class and comfortable, a place where nothing ever happens, just before dinnertime on a school night in mid-September, a week and a bit into a first term that looked like it had the potential to really suck. I was gazing into a mirror. Dylan Maples was staring back. He had black, disheveled hair that a comb would only enter at its peril, a white face so forgettable that God likely couldn't recognize it, and all sorts of other features that I would most definitely classify as faults.

I was sick of him.

"Who are you?"

He didn't answer me.

I swear his eye bags were getting darker every day. Eye bags at fifteen and three-quarters. Does that even make any sense?

I used to think that Dylan Maples was kind of a cool guy. Back in the day, he had a pretty wicked sense of humor, parental units who actually didn't tick him off, and four important friends; and of those friends, if I were to venture to say it out loud, he may have been the coolest. The others were no slouches either, at least in Dylan Maples's mind. We had had a lot of fun over the years.

That is all over now. In fact, one of us is completely over. Dead. Bought the farm. Met his maker. Gone for a long run off a short dock.

"Hey, wait a minute, that's not entirely true." Bomber was sitting on the edge of my bed. He looked exactly the way he used to when he was alive. I ignored him. He hates that.

"Dinner!"

Hark, a voice from below: John Maples, dear old Dad, down in the kitchen helping Laura Maples make a healthy meal, heavy on the vegetables. Ah, the parental units, individuals charged with trying to steer me in the right direction in what seems to me is a pretty confusing world right now. Every time I check out anything on social media—and I'll admit that I do that a bit—everyone seems to have such strong opinions and it feels like they are constantly broadcasting them. Even kids my age appear to have really developed social and even political positions. I always wonder what I should say, or if I should say anything. I want to be a good person. I don't want anybody to think I'm a jerk, but it is hard to keep up sometimes. I worry that my opinions aren't strong enough, or at least the opinions of Dylan Maples—the guy who represents me in life—aren't. In fact, he doesn't seem to have powerful views about anything. However, I do have a vast array of sarcastic comments I can unleash at a second's notice.

"Coming!" I shouted back.

That is a key word for kids my age. Very useful. It means *I will be there when I feel like it*, even when Mom and Pops are working their butts off to prepare food for us, food to give us life that their hard-earned coinage purchased. Most parents will tell you how much they do for their kids the second you ask them. Maybe that's a little too cynical. Mom and Dad do a lot for me, a whole lot, though that sort of thing is hard to admit sometimes. Mostly, I would rather just be a kid, at least a little rebellious, and keep the gratitude hidden. "I'LL BE THERE WHEN I FEEL LIKE IT!" That's what

I actually should have yelled. I don't have the stones to do that, though. Dylan Maples doesn't, and I'm stuck being him.

"Dylan!"

Girls.

There are three of them I think about. To be honest, I think about them a lot. And two of them are actually real. Maybe I reflect on them too much. I don't know. I don't mean anything by it, but nevertheless, I do it.

Dylan Maples gave me a bit of a smirk in the mirror. Stop that. Smart aleck. Appear calm and collected, that's a better look.

"There's only one of you, dude," said Bomber with a sigh.

I ignored him again and examined myself a little closer, and as I did, I realized that some girls might consider me somewhat handsome, if they looked beyond the pimples, the disheveled hair, and the pasty skin. Handsome: that's not the word they would use, if they were to consider me okay. They'd say "cute." But quite a few girls these days say that looks don't matter anyway. So, why do they talk about "cute guys" then?

I don't know. They're hard to understand.

Maybe they are talking about deeper things; things beyond looks. Is that really the way girls think? Or is that just a social position? Do I have those deeper things, the things they like?

"Dylan!" Dad for a third time, this time a little louder.

"Coming!"

It seems to me that the reason I think about these three girls so much—the two real ones and the imaginary one—is that they are far away. I don't have to actually see them in person. That would be difficult. I can't think of a single girl in my school who I would want to take me seriously. That would be perilous. But the far-away girls, they're cool.

"Dylan, your meal will be cold if you don't come now!"

The first girl I think about lives in northern Ontario, in one of what they call the "Tri-Towns" up there. Cobalt. No one has ever heard of it. I hadn't, until I went up there with lawyer-dad so he could try to solve a problem that turned into a sort of mystery that I got involved in. You wouldn't think there would be mysteries or excitement of any sort in Cobalt, but there most definitely are.

Actually, you wouldn't think there's much mystery or excitement in Canada, period. It's got that sort of vanilla reputation. But there is. Canada is weird. Trust me. It pretends it isn't, but underneath, this country is bat-crap crazy. It's like an iceberg, with a cool surface and all sorts of invisible things going on underneath.

Wynona Dixon. That's her name. I know, it sounds like a fictional name. She is kind of fictional in my mind too, kind of perfect. Wyn Dixon, with long, wavy blonde hair and the heart of a lioness, both as a hockey player—and I should know; I went up against her back when I played hockey—and off the ice. It's been a few years since I saw her, but I remember her as if it were yesterday, walking along those frozen Cobalt streets in her bright-red coat, her face glowing in the cold, looking as if she would like to hold my hand, full of spirit. A spirit I wish I had now. We keep in touch, text all the time. She sends me pictures every now and then. She looks really good. Grown up. I think I might suck out if I had to talk to her in person, though.

"That's stupid, Dylan," said Bomber.

Then there's Dorothy Osborne. Sounds fictional too. Very different from Wyn, but kind of the same too. Reddish-brown hair, she wears kind of old-fashioned movie-costume things, not afraid of looking different, even puts her hair in pigtails sometimes. She lives in Drumheller, Alberta. That's where I met her, when me and my guys got lost with her in Dinosaur Provincial Park and nearly got preyed upon by a weirdo criminal called The Reptile. She wishes she didn't live in Drumheller, thinks it's Nowheresville, but I thought it was pretty cool. I text her all the time, too.

Finally, there's Alice. Alice in Wonderland. She doesn't really exist. I dreamt her up right after I met Dorothy, when I went to British Columbia—wonderland—with Mom and Dad to recover from what happened in Alberta. She had a thing for wild makeup, a really forthright way about her that hid some insecurities, and a tattoo of a unicorn on her hip and a ring in her belly button. Uh, saw them when we were at the beach—or in my dream of her. I dreamed up a whole adventure in Sasquatch Provincial Park out there in BC, with Alice as my leading lady. There really is a place called that, in weird Canada. I was running around with her chasing after a sasquatch… in my dream. Then I went there, and it was unbelievable, actually like something you would make up.

"I like weird," I imagined Alice said to me once, peering right into my eyes. That made me feel good.

"Dylan!" yelled Mom.

When Mom starts yelling then I'm really in trouble. She operates a private school here in Toronto, runs a tight ship. She can be tough and makes fun of me quite a bit, but she likes to hug a lot too, which is kind of annoying. At least that's the position I take publicly.

"Dylan, you should go," said Bomber. "You spend too much time in your room now, anyway. You don't talk to anyone much either. When was the last time you hung out with Rhett or Jason or Terry?"

"Quiet, Bomb," I whispered, "you don't understand."

"I understand that when they text you now, you don't even answer."

"I'm putting your food away in ten seconds!" shouted Mom.

So, these three girls. When I text them, they text back, or at least Wyn and Dorothy do. They are definitely supportive. They both even told me that they loved me when I told them about Bomb dying. Down at the end of each of their messages, they wrote: "Love you. Wyn" and "Love from me, D." I remember exactly how they both put it. Alice's was the best, but I don't like to repeat what she said...of course, she didn't actually say it because she doesn't exist. I made up a number for her and text it every now and then, but don't actually send it...I would be an even bigger twit than I am if I did that. She has said the most amazing things to me. Really gets you in the old ticker.

I rolled out of the room and took the stairs three at a time, turned the corner, and got into the kitchen in about three seconds from bedroom departure, left

Bomb in my dust. Likely a new world record. The room was empty. What? Had they abandoned me? Probably a good move on their part.

"Out here, honey," said Mom. They were sitting at the table in the dining room.

I wish she wouldn't call me that, and why were they eating out there? This didn't bode well. We only eat out there when we have guests, when Mom cleans the house for about five hours ahead of time and Dad gets out the good wine, or on special family occasions.

"Why are we out here?"

John Maples was at the head of the table, of course. Mom lets him do that. She was down at the same end as him to his right and my meal, all hot and steaming, not cold in the least, was close to them, right across from her. It was a lovely little Maples family gathering.

"No reason," said Mom, smiling.

That was even worse. When she says a line like that, I know something is up. Dad gave me a smile. Oh, God. This was suspiciously like the time they told me we were going to Cobalt.

"Have a seat, champ."

He still calls me that. Can't believe it. Do I really have to tell him not to do it?

"Love you," said Mom.

All right, they must be sending me to Siberia.

"Eat up," said Dad, "your mom and I spent a long time on this meal."

She smirked, which meant that she had done most of the work and he was taking credit for a chunk of it. I can't complain about their relationship though, my parents really love each other. I know that sounds strange. I know maybe a half-dozen kids in my entire class who have parents who are still together, and most of them, from the way they look at each other when they pick those kids up from school, aren't long for this world as teams. My Mom and Dad hug each other a lot, and kiss too, right in front of me. I try not to look. Not that they don't argue. They do, and she always wins. He's a lawyer, and she smokes him just about every time. Even when he's trying his best to be all open-minded and liberal, which he actually is, but sometimes he really puts on a pro-feminist sort of thing to score points. Not that he's not pro-feminist. He is.

"I want you to know," he has told me about a million times when we've been alone, starting when I was about twelve, "that one of the most important things in life is how you treat women...or...girls."

"Yes, Dad."

Usually we were watching a hockey game, Mom was out doing something, Dad had made pizza, and we were "batching it." His words.

"You never ever, ever, ever, ever, under any circumstances, hit a woman—a girl—do you understand?"

"Yeah, sure Dad, of course. Why would I do that? That would be gross. And stupid."

"Look at me."

I looked at him.

"It doesn't matter what they've done or how upset they might make you. You respect women—uh, girls—you treat them...."

I forget the rest, even though he's said it to me about a billion times. But he's right. I think that how you treat the opposite sex says something about who you are... not that I know who the heck I am. I wish I had someone like Wyn or D or Alice—especially Alice—to treat the right way. Perhaps that's a little needy at fifteen and a... almost sixteen?

I got through that dining-room meal in about, oh, I'd say two to three minutes. One hundred and twenty seconds, maybe one-forty and it was gone, down the hatch. It had been a Laura Maples specialty with a little meat on its bones: roast chicken, corn, mashed potatoes and gravy, and a little ice cream for dessert.

There were no disturbances, either. Bomber hadn't followed me downstairs and wasn't sitting there at the far end of the table like he's done a few times, actually daring to appear in public, his ghostliness eyeballing me and wondering when we were going out to play street hockey. He has kind of replaced Grandpa in the ghost department. My awesome grandfather, who loved hockey just like me, died a few years ago. I still see him in my dreams sometimes. I sort of feel the presence of people from my past. Bizarre, I know. But neither Bomber nor Grandpa made a peep during this meal and I was grateful for that. I jumped to my feet: back up to my room and my phone.

"Uh, wait a minute, champ."

Uh-oh. There *is* something up. This meal was a bribe.

"We need to talk with you."

"Uh, can it wait, Mom?"

"No."

She usually isn't quite that decisive with me about things. She usually gives what I might term lots of leeway in her comments to and about me, giving me "my space," as she says. My Mom and Dad are weird (though I suppose that goes without saying about parents). They are children of the sixties...even though they weren't even born back then, in fact, they were about minus fifteen or twenty, but they like all the "groovy" bands from those days, and kind of have a "love generation" attitude. Both Mom and Dad are really successful, smart at their jobs, and efficient, but they believe in hope and peace and all that crap. I shouldn't say that. They are obviously right for the most part...but still, it's kind of weird.

"We, uh, have some concerns about you," said Mom.

Oh, man, here we go. I have really changed, that's what they are going to say; I have become much quieter, my marks aren't as good, I'm still grieving for Bomb, most kids don't lose close friends in head-on collisions at my age, and I maybe should have gone to the other high school, the Catholic one where all my friends went, Rhett Norton, Jason Li, and Terry Singh, the buds, old hockey teammates. And by the way, Dylan, why did you give up hockey? It isn't even late September yet, you could still sign up. And why do you spend all your time on your phone and in your room now?

Of course, I don't spend ALL my time there—or on my phone—just some of it. I suppose I could use my phone to call my friends sometimes. I'm fine, though. But Mom and Dad tell me this stuff constantly. It never goes anywhere. They don't understand.

They have lots of views about so-called millennials too, all people their age do. I'm not even sure I qualify as a millennial, but they think I do and man do they get lots of mileage out of it. Our music sucks, we are self-centered, so "presentist" (whatever that means), we're always on social media, we are spoiled, blah, blah, blah. They don't exactly say that, my mom and dad aren't like that, but it's what they mean, behind their words. It is like a subtle war on us. Judge John Maples and his wife Judge Laura, hitting you hard but pretending to be friendly...and fair, of course.

I waited until they'd gotten it all out. That's all you have to do, allow them to let off a little steam, and then say you kind of get it, or act mad at them (they don't like that; worries them) and then just go on with your life.

This time, though, they threw a curveball.

"We are planning a family trip," said Dad.

"Eh?"

"A family trip," said Mom. "A family is a group of related people. And a trip is a journey across a section of the earth or a body of water."

We hadn't done one of those for a long while. We used to do them all the time. The first one was to Newfoundland to an amazing place that really fit my imagination: a deserted town on an island called

Ireland's Eye. That may have been where my dead-people thing really ramped up because I actually saw someone like that there, I think. The trip to northern Ontario where I met Wyn and the one to Alberta where I got to know Dorothy were "family" things too, and the BC trip where I met—or made up—You Know Who.

"Well, good luck with that," I said, with a smile. "When are you going? Can I stay home alone?"

"We," said Mom.

"Eh?"

"We," repeated Dad. These two like to work as a team on you. "WE are going together, you and Mom and me. Next week. Heading out on Saturday, to be exact."

Today was Thursday, just a day away from Friday. I was counting the now just under twenty-four hours until I could settle into a nice weekend. I was only a week and a half into grade ten. It was not going well. Lousy, really. I wasn't optimistic about making new friends this year. Not that I had any of real value last year either. And the girls, man they looked awesome. They seemed more awesome every year, which was both a good and a bad thing. But how were WE going on this family trip, if I had to be in school?

"We are pulling you out of classes for the week, maybe ten days. We think it will do you good."

"Right." It didn't make any sense. I was pretty sure they'd get over this in a couple of days. There was no way they would really pull me out of school.

"We just think," continued Mom, "that it would be nice for us all to get away for a while, together, regardless of what else is happening in our lives. I am taking time away from my own school and your father has told his clients that he is incommunicado for a little while. He will be leaving his phone behind, and so will I. Right, John?"

"Yes…yes, absolutely, Mom."

I hate it when he calls her that.

"It will just be the three of us on the trip out. We will have time to talk and when we get to where we are going, an amazing, quiet, beautiful place where we will be with friends, we'll have some time there too."

"So, where are we going?" Really, if I were to tell the truth, I should have said, "Where do you *think* we are going?"

"Uh…" said Dad.

"To New Brunswick," said Mom

"…New Brunswick?"

So, remember when I said Canada is weird? There are some exceptions.

Nothing weird ever happens in New Brunswick.

2

CALM BEFORE THE STORM

Okay, I was wrong, I went with them. They made me go. I had no choice, mostly because Mom refused to cook anything and leave it behind for me. When I was putting up a fuss about going with them, she basically cleaned out the fridge and then let me have a look at it. It was terrifying. I could feel my stomach rumbling just staring at it. I don't have any money either. I used to have a job in a fast food place, but I quit. Bad decision, because not being gainfully employed has put me at the mercy of the parental units for funds. So, unless I wanted to starve for the ten days they were gone, I had to go with them.

And to be honest, deep down, I think I wanted to go. Can't explain that one.

Dad used to have a Jeep and Mom had a mid-sized Toyota. Now they both have hybrids, little cars that give me about as much leg room in the back seat as an NBA player in a matchbox. I'm kind of built like a stork right now anyway, legs about twice the length of the rest of me. This has only been the case for maybe six months. I'm growing like a weed. My feet look like pontoons on the end of my legs and I trip over just about anything and run into everything. Sometimes I wake up in the morning and swear I'm a foot taller than when I went to bed. It's like I'm a monster in a Guillermo del Toro movie. I can eat anything at any time of any day. I can pulverize a snack that Mom has left out for me, then destroy an entire meal, seconds and thirds included, and then inhale a couple of bowls of cereal about half an hour later. I might be exaggerating a bit, but I need fuel, constantly.

Maybe the toughest thing about the trip was being without my phone. Well, I actually wasn't without it and neither were Mom and Dad. We all brought our phones. They were just out of reach. All three were in airplane mode, imprisoned in the glove compartment like a full-course meal sitting just out of the reach of three starving people. Well, one at least. Though I'm pretty sure that before we were even out of Toronto,

Mom and Dad were ready to tear the friggin' cover off the glove compartment to see what the heck was happening on their phones.

But they pretended they weren't thinking about it at all. I'd never seen them go for more than half an hour without looking at their screens, a fact that they would deny, since they were so caught up in how much I, the stupid "millennial," was constantly on his. They had all sorts of theories about the effect these devilish little apparatuses had on my generation, what they were doing to our social skills and our imaginations and all that, but I swear Dad was glancing over at the glove compartment every few minutes. On the surface, he and Mom acted as if all was normal. Actually, it was hyper-normal, disgustingly, perfectly normal, like a scene from a 1970s family sitcom.

"So, Dylan, tell me a bit about some of your friends this year," said Dad.

"Uh, just getting started at school this term, Dad. Haven't really met anyone new yet."

I had my head pressed against the window trying with everything I had not to be bored right out of my skull or just fall asleep. The suburbs east of Toronto were passing by and Mom and Dad had some Beatles, Rolling Stones, and James Brown playing. Groovy. I had a map on the seat beside me—a paper one, a relic from a different time—that Dad had given me to follow where we were going. He is into that sort of thing, likes to know exactly where he is at all times, likes to know how far it is to each place we are going, the population of all the towns and cities, all that stuff. I must admit, I'm a bit like that too, don't know why. Mom couldn't care less. I guess she figures we will get where we are going without having to know the distance to each place and everything about it. She'd rather talk about real things going on in our lives. Gag me. That was what bothered me about Dad's question; he doesn't usually ask me that sort of thing.

"Let's talk about Thomas's death," Mom said.

That's what she calls Bomb. He was my winger, both in hockey and in life. Bomb Connors was an emotional guy sometimes, not always the brightest bulb in the candelabra, but a really good guy. Someone I wish now I'd talked to more—really talked to, if you know what I mean. He bought it in a head-on collision on the 401. He was driving with another kid who hadn't had his license for very long and some guy going the wrong way on the highway ran into them. *Poof*. It was all over. It was pretty tough to deal with, but I think Mom and Dad make too big a deal about it. I'm just going through some things right now, being in a new school and losing Bomb. I'll get over it.

"Let's not," I said.

"There is no use in keeping it all inside," said Mom.

"First of all, there is some use in that, trust me, and there isn't really a lot I'm keeping inside anyway."

"Sometimes," said Dad, "guys like to keep things to—"

"Oh, don't give me that manly crap, you two. It's not healthy."

There was silence for a while.

"Hey!" said Dad suddenly, as if he had just discovered insulin, "Kingston is the next place up ahead. You know, it was once nearly named the capital of Canada and the first Prime Minister came from here!" It went on from there. He launched into another one of his monologues. He is given to that kind of thing. Mom and I used to call his speeches the "John Maples Lectures." We never told him. It was kind of our joke, together.

I didn't like the long stretches when there wasn't much happening outside my window. Lately, silence and boredom had become my enemies. I start thinking too much, and about the wrong things. That was usually when Bomber appeared, and a couple of times on that road trip he did, sitting in the back seat hoping I would talk to him, sometimes looking kind of smashed up from his accident. I tried hard to keep staring out the window whenever he showed up. The drive from Kingston to the Quebec border, without a single stop and just kilometre after kilometre of highway, was difficult.

"Hey, man," Bomb finally said just east of Cornwall, "say something. Tell your parents how you're feeling. Open up. I died. It happens."

"Go away," I said in my mind. "No, don't go away. Just...don't bother me about this."

I remembered the day of the accident. Bomber's mom actually called to tell us. I was home alone. She started to cry, told me all about the funeral arrangements. I think I said, "okay." That was it. I didn't go, of course.

As the kilometres passed, Mom tried to tease me into talking a few times, telling me to "please keep it down and give the others a chance to say something." I wouldn't bite, though.

I was glad when we got to Montreal, where we stopped for the night and stayed in a nice "boutique" hotel right downtown. They took me out for crêpes and a very Montreal-type meal in a café on one of those very Montreal-type streets where you can sit outside and eat and you hear French in the air, and it's almost like the city is trying to tell you how much cooler it is than Toronto. Mom didn't try asking me about Bomb again.

"You know what I think," said Dad, as he set his fork down after polishing off a chocolate-and-strawberry special, "I think it's just great not to have my phone at my beck and call all the time. I really do. I'm getting used to it. It makes you want to talk to others. Being social is just so important in life, a great tonic!"

Of course, really, he was just telling me how he thinks I should act. It was pretty obvious. He seemed a little jumpy, actually. Phone withdrawal.

THE NEXT DAY WE didn't drive too far, just to Quebec City. We stayed at another boutique hotel and then visited the Old City, the whole place like a throwback to the 1700s, and there was even more French in the air and more outdoor cafés and it seemed as if Quebec City was trying to tell us how much cooler it was than Montreal. That's a Canadian thing. We are like a whole bunch of siblings always competing with each other. A family though, definitely a family.

The parental units kept trying to get me to talk. It was like they were hoping I was suddenly going to just pour out all my emotions and admit to all sorts of inadequacies and say I was going to do better in the future.

"So, how do you like this?" asked Mom as we strolled along the wide boardwalk in the sunshine near this awesome old hotel called the Château Frontenac. It definitely looked like a castle. We could see out over the St. Lawrence River.

"Nice," I said.

"And?"

"Nice," I repeated.

"Hey!" said Dad, "you know, this hotel was one of a chain of great railway hotels built across Canada. They put this baby up in 1893."

"Okay."

They hate one-word answers.

"And this up here and kind of down below us is the Plains of Abraham. That was a where the fate of Canada got decided in 1759 in a gigantic battle between the French and the English. There was this guy named General Wolfe for the English and Montcalm for the French, and the redcoats came up the St. Lawrence over there." Dad stopped and pointed up river. "They attacked the French and somehow climbed up the sheer cliffs below the fort right here and everyone just went at it, muskets and cannons blazing, bayonets out and hacking each other."

Now that sounded amazing.

"That's pretty awesome," I admitted. Three words. Mom put her hand on my shoulder. I could just imagine that battle. I am pretty good at imagining things. I guess my face lit up a little. I leaned over the railing and looked down at the cliff. "I can almost hear the guns going off," I said. "I wonder what it would really sound like. The soldiers would probably be crying out, wounded, and dying and all. It would likely sound pretty bizarre, the bullets zipping through the air, sucking into flesh, limbs getting sheared off, that sort of thing."

Dad smiled at me. Mom did not.

"Violence never really solves anything," she said. "Can we either talk about something else or at least tone down the blood and gore a bit?"

Party pooper.

THE NEXT DAY, WE drove all the rest of the way to New Brunswick. We got up early, headed toward Rivière du Loup and then plunged down out of Quebec, past this place called St. Louis de Ha-Ha! I am not making that up—and the exclamation mark is part of the name, too.

As I said, Canada is weird.

We swept across the border into New Brunswick, past this little town called Edmunston and then swung east to go straight across the province toward the town of Bathurst on Chaleur Bay. That was where we were going to stay, with some friends of my parents' from Toronto. These people had "given it all up," moved out east, and had been bugging Mom and Dad to visit them ever since.

The landscape got awfully boring awfully quickly. It was a bit interesting at first, kind of hilly, nearly mountainous. I had no idea there was anything even remotely like mountains in New Brunswick. Mostly, though, it was just trees. Evergreen, coniferous, whatever you call them. Trees and trees and trees and trees and trees and trees and trees and trees. It was so mind-numbing that Bomber didn't even show up and I fell asleep. This wasn't very promising. Even New Brunswick could not be this boring. It was like being in some sort of tunnel and I would come to my senses and then fade again, just waiting to surface at the other side. The only thing of any interest were these yellow signs with drawings of moose and cars on them...indicating that one of those bad boys might suddenly appear out of the fifty billion acres of trees and total your car...and you. Kind of cool.

Finally, after a couple of hours, which seemed like about fifteen days, we emerged into semi-farmland and a few houses and finally we came to the city of Bathurst, though "city" is a very generous word. There wasn't much to it.

It was early afternoon. We stopped in at a Tim Hortons and grabbed some donuts and the parental units loaded up on coffee. I saw an old comedy skit once on TV with these guys dressed like typical Canadians, talking hockey and drinking beer, and wearing toques and named Doug and Bob McKenzie. Pretty funny. Well, everyone in this place looked like they were either them, or their wives or girlfriends, or related to them. It also seemed that everyone could speak both French and English. There were lots of people saying "eh" too, and being friendly and holding doors for other people. On the streets, they even stopped for pedestrians to cross in front of a car. In Toronto, every one of them would have been a corpse the second they tried that.

We drove around a little after that so Dad could "show me the town." That didn't take very long. Even the big arena didn't get me too excited, despite the fact that they have a Quebec Major Junior League team that plays in it, called the Acadie-Bathurst Titan. Kind of a cool name. Hockey is in my past now, though.

All the signs in town were in both languages and for some reason there were also placards everywhere for local political parties.

"I didn't know there was an election happening," I said.

Mom was happy to explain. "It must be for a by-election, honey, one that takes place when a member of parliament dies or retires suddenly. This looks like a federal one."

There were blue signs for the Conservatives, red for the Liberals, orange for the NDP, and green for the Greens. But there were also lots of blue, red, and white signs promoting an "Independent" candidate, too. In fact, he had by far the most. I figured he was going to win. Maybe he and his gang were just better at getting lots of their stuff onto lawns. Theirs said things like, "VOTE FOR A REAL LOCAL GUY," and "A FRIEND, A NEIGHBOUR, NOT A POLITICIAN," or "KEEP ACADIE-BATHURST FOR ACADIE-BATHURST," and "NO MORE ELITES!" The candidate was this guy named Jim Fiat and there were lots of pictures of him on his signs. He had perfectly combed blond hair, a big smile, and kind of looked like a salesman to me.

Things appeared pretty working-class in town; it didn't seem like they had too much money here. Then we headed out of the downtown area to the place we were going to stay. We drove through the suburbs, then out toward the water and saw the flat blue surface of

Chaleur Bay, which was like a thick finger poking into the land out of the Gulf of St. Lawrence.

We passed a fancy looking golf course and the houses started getting bigger and nicer, much nicer when we got near the beach and moved along a road that was parallel to the water. Dad was now leaning forward in the driver's seat looking for the house. Despite myself, I started to get interested.

"Who are these people, again?" I asked.

Mom turned around and smiled at me, obviously thrilled that I was "engaging" for the second time in a short while. "Bill and Bonnie," she said. "I don't know if you remember them, but they used to live in Moore Park, about five doors down from us. Moved to the States for a while, and then came here."

"No."

"You were only little."

"Is it just them?" I was hoping for the smallest group of hosts as possible.

"Yes. They're wonderful. You'll love them."

"Why?"

Mom paused. "Well, they are nice people. Bonnie's first husband died, so Bill is her second, a bit older than she is, married him not long before they left Toronto. We don't know him quite as well as her. He's a sort of self-help guru for businesses, interesting to talk with, written a bunch of books, been an advisor to all sorts of corporations, helps them be better, treat their employees better. He makes sure they take a holistic approach and are good citizens."

"And make more money," added Dad, squinting in the sun as he looked for numbers on the big houses. The buildings were almost all on our right side, where the bay was—the other side of the street was simply a forest of evergreen trees. This place reminded me of the pictures I had seen of the Hamptons on Long Island, not far from New York, where rich people and celebrities lived out in the country, near the water, their version of roughing it. These New Brunswick residences weren't as wealthy-looking as the ones in the Hamptons, and this area was more Canadian in terms of the trees that were around, but the vibe was similar—big weathered houses on the beach, little trails going down to the water—rustic, that's the word...rustic for people with money.

"They just had one kid—a girl, from Bonnie's first marriage—though she and Bill are apparently really close," continued Mom. "She's about eight or ten years older than you, I think she's doing ballet or something in L.A. now. Bonnie is a sweetheart, does lots of things for charities, and absolutely loves dogs."

"You've got that right, Mom," said Dad. "I think she has about thirteen of them."

"Four."

"She kisses them right on the mouth and calls them sweetie and darling and that sort of thing."

Gag me.

"Bill and Bonnie are lovely," repeated Mom, "and they were so kind to invite us to stay here for a week."

Oh, God, a week with an old guy who pretends he's helping others but really is just making the big bucks so he can have a smoking summer place on Chaleur Bay.

"They live here permanently now; said they were sick of the city."

So, too many people get on this guy's nerves. Teach people how to be good to each other, but stay away from people, generally. Dogs though, they are fine.

"Here it is," said Dad.

3

THE BILL AND BONNIE SHOW

Dad pulled into a gravel driveway in front of a home that I had to admit looked awesome. It was a big wood-frame house three storeys high with gables on the top floor, painted forest green and with lots of windows offering views both onto the road on one side, and out over the water and beach on the other. You could see right through the house in places.

A woman was standing near the front door surrounded by dogs, four of them, all golden retrievers from what I could tell. She had short blonde hair that I think was dyed and was dressed simply in jeans and a T-shirt, but you could see that these "casual" clothes were the best of their kind. Rich people these days dress like that all the time. "I am not better than you. I am an ordinary person. I am casual. I have no airs…but these jeans, they cost four-hundred and fifty dollars. I'll tell you all about it, if you want to hear." As we came to a halt, a man walked out to join her. He was dressed the same, except his T-shirt had a Toronto Raptors logo on it, the Drake tee, black-and-gold, expensive kind. Funny thing about this couple—they both wore glasses and had another pair, reading glasses, I suppose, hanging from their necks.

The woman gave a little shriek and extended her arms to Mom as they rushed toward each other and then they hugged it out for a long time, this woman saying how much she had missed Mom. Dad and Bill did a manly hug and slapped each other on the back. Then they all turned to me.

"This is Dylan," said Mom.

"Well, aren't you a grown-up young man!" said Bonnie. "The last time I saw you, you must have been two feet shorter."

They all laughed. I did not. There was a slight pause.

"Hey, pal, how is it going?" asked Bill. "Whazz up?"

He actually said that. I felt like responding "Not much, bro. I'll fill you in on the down-low on my life in a while. Nice crib!" Instead, I just said. "Not much. Thank you for inviting us to stay with you."

"My, what a polite young fellow," said Bonnie.

"Not a problem, my man," said Bill. "Come on in! You've got a bedroom all to yourself, top floor, looking out over the water."

Guest rooms for at least three visitors? And this was just their "summer place" at one point?

"Make yourselves at home," said Bonnie as we came in. The vestibule was huge and it opened up into a massive open-concept main floor with nearly floor-to-ceiling windows that made the place incredibly bright. You could look out and see people passing by along the beach. Beyond it, the blue water stretched out flat like a giant hockey rink, hilly green shorelines on two sides and going out forever in the middle. There was a big deck out back too. It was all pretty cool. The only problem with this house was that it was so open-concept that there wasn't any place to be on your own. To hide.

They took us to our rooms. Mine was impressive, I must admit. The view was to kill for. I dropped my duffle bag on the floor and lay on the bed. I could hear the adults talking in the distance. I didn't want to go downstairs, just wanted to lie there. I found myself reaching for my phone several times. What the heck was I going to do here for a whole week? I envisioned endless walks on the beach with the parental units, delving into my problems. I sure hoped Bill wasn't going to work on me.

When they called me for what they termed a "late lunch," I couldn't rely on the "coming!" trick. That would have been rude and I am a Canadian, after all.

I checked out the living room and dining room as I strolled toward the big wooden table they were all sitting at, smiling at me. There were lots of books on shelves—mostly about art, architecture, and business— lots of flowers on display, a connecting kitchen with a long island and full of stainless-steel appliances and copper-coloured (rustic) pots and other things hanging from the walls. The walls weren't painted, just "fatigued" (I think that's the right word) to look as if they hadn't been touched at all…casual.

Bill turned to Dad as I approached. "The main beach is beautiful here," he said, "Youghall Beach." He pronounced it very carefully, as if only an expert would know how to say it right, as if only the locals, those in the know, could do it. It sounded almost like "U-Haul."

The conversation around that "rustic" wood table wasn't in the least bit interesting. Though Bill, who was about seventy and had white hair—and who looked a little emaciated to me, likely from eating too many vegetables and having some work done on his face—kept trying to ask me questions that I think he thought would lead to me imagining he was cool. He asked about the music I listened to, about the Raptors and Toronto FC (not a word about the Leafs), and video games I played. He dropped a few names of singers, tunes, players, and games. Most of them were pretty lame, but I didn't let on, of course.

"Dylan is a hockey player," said Dad.

"Was," amended Mom.

"Oh," said Bonnie and didn't add anything, though her face showed a bit of disdain.

"I am not a hockey fan," announced Bill, "too violent a sport, and the hockey parents, they are awful. So competitive, always screaming at their kids. We put Abigail in soccer."

"Yes," said Bonnie, "and we loved that, used to take our lawn chairs to the games and watch. The parents were civilized about things, for the most part. It was about team and exercise, that sort of idea, being good sports. There wasn't the sort of violence you see at the hockey rink."

"Have you ever been in a hockey rink?" I blurted out. I knew the second I said it, that I shouldn't have. We studied a bit of psychology in school, learned about

Sigmund Freud and Carl Jung. I think that was what one of them would have called my "id"—my animal, unfiltered self—speaking. I immediately clammed up and there was silence for a moment.

"No, actually," Bonnie finally said with a bit of a forced smile.

"You don't need to," said Bill. "All you have to do is watch it on television. It seems to me that hockey feeds into the whole passive-aggressive thing that Canadians have in their psyche, a bit disturbing, if you ask me."

Wait, I thought, *aren't YOU a Canadian*?

"Dylan just liked to play," said Mom. "He liked to test himself when the games were close, see if he had what it took in a sport that was fast and a little rough at times, and awfully exciting."

I almost stood and kissed her, but there was silence again.

"Well, each to their own, I say!" said Bill, "that's the beauty of life."

"We like sports that give you an outdoors kind of exercise," said Bonnie. "We like to sail and to canoe."

Ah yes, I thought, *I should have brought my yacht.*

"If I have to watch team sports," chimed in Bill, "I'll watch basketball or soccer, European athletics. Less aggressive encounters."

"No competition in those ones," I said sarcastically. I had done it again. My blinkin' id! The words had just burst out of me. I also wanted to add that it was a good thing he was against competition...being a guy who coaches businesses. Thankfully, however, I just kept my comments to that first inappropriate thing.

Bill laughed, though I thought the laugh was a little hollow. It was as if he had calculated it was time for a little levity, a perfect tool to put me at ease, a technique to use on people to make them more open to you and accepting of your opinions. He seemed awfully calculating generally.

Then he steered the conversation to other things, as if he'd had enough of this snot-nosed kid, though of course he didn't make much of an effort to include me in the rest of the talk. He made a big point of saying that he didn't watch any television, though they had an enormous flat-screen TV in their "library" and I'd noticed another on the wall in their bedroom (and hadn't he said something about watching sports on television?). He was one of those "I don't watch TV" adults. You hear them all the time. I tried to concentrate on the food. There was lots of quinoa and zucchini and that sort of thing.

Bill had a million theories about people and society, and Dad and Mom tried to keep up with him. His thoughts were different from theirs, though. He seemed to think, deep down, that he was absolutely right about everything, even though he tried to give the impression that he was completely open-minded and what he was saying were really just opinions about culture and human beings. Mom and Dad never came off like that. They did try to keep up with the discussion, though, and sound polite.

"Is there an election going on here?" asked Mom. "We noticed all the signs on the way in."

Oh, man, I thought, *now here's a scintillating subject.*

"There is indeed," said Bill, "and I'm glad you brought that up."

"Bill has some interesting ideas about this one," said Bonnie, smiling at Mom, looking as if she'd really like to talk about almost anything else. Bonnie and I were actually on the same page for a few minutes.

"I've always been a Liberal, John," said Bill to my Dad, "even a socialist when I was younger. But sometimes I actually agree with a few of the Conservatives. I bet you never would have guessed that! You must think outside of the box sometimes. There's a fellow by the name of Jim Fiat running for parliament here—a new kind of Conservative, an Independent, so he isn't tied to the old parties and old ways. He calls himself a man of the people. That usually makes me laugh, especially coming out of the mouth of a right-winger. You remember what Prime Minister Pierre Trudeau said? 'There is no one older than a young Conservative.'"

They all laughed at that.

"But," said Bill, "this chap has me thinking a little bit. He really is for the people, it seems to me, or at least in his muddling kind of way. He answers his own phone if you call him, and he is concerned about the 'elites' running everything. He says he is going to go to Ottawa to truly speak for the little guy. He wants to change things. And it looks like he's going to win."

I thought that "elites" comment was a strange one for Bill to make. If you really can call some people "elites," he seemed like one to me.

"I think we sometimes get too complicated about life, my friends," added Bill. "This man is offering a simple message. It is kind of: 'what you see is what you get.' You don't have to look below the surface with him. I think I like that."

I was bored out of my mind. Bill continued to look thrilled with his own ideas, but I thought they were more like sleeping pills. The "late lunch" had gone to past mid-afternoon. Finally, I asked if I might be excused. There was silence again.

"Sure, honey," said Bonnie. "Make yourself at home."

Honey, again. I may be a lot of things, but I'm not honey.

Mom gave me a bit of a longing look, but I just got up, excused myself, and headed to my room.

After about an hour of listening to them talking in the distance as I stared out over the dark-blue Chaleur Bay and imagined just sailing away on it, I decided to go outside. I was worried that if I stayed there too long Bomber might show up. I had noticed a back door at the bottom of the stairs up to our rooms that I could access without having to walk past the adults.

THE SEA AIR FELT great on my face as I made my way down the little wooden boardwalk beside Bill and Bonnie's house, past their huge deck, and headed to the beach. It was getting late and the sun would soon set. The beach wasn't particularly wide and it was far from perfect. Rustic. That would fit. It wasn't like some perfect tropical beach or one in the US, in Florida or California. It was a bit muddy and had lots of stones, driftwood, and seashells. There weren't many people on it and the few I saw kind of reminded me of Bill and Bonnie, many of them wearing khaki shorts and expensive-looking tops and sandals. The houses nearby were big like our hosts' place. I moved in one direction for a while and then turned and walked the other way, toward Bathurst, which I could see in the distance. I took my time, wandering around, not wanting to return to the adults and their conversation. Eventually, I came to a sign that read "Youghall Beach" and then there were other signs about swimming and proper conduct. Obviously, this was a place where the townspeople and tourists came to swim in numbers, though now it was late in the day and later in the year. There were just a few more people in this area.

I stopped at one point, turned to the water, and just stared out at it. After a while, I realized someone was doing the same thing about fifty metres away. It was a girl. She had long, black, curly hair. It struck me that she kind of resembled Alice. She turned and looked at me. I looked away, back out over the water.

Then she started walking toward me.

4

ANTONINE

I was wrong. She wasn't coming toward me. I had been standing a bit closer to the water than her and she was focused on something out in the bay. What it was, I couldn't tell. She came to a stop about the distance from the blue-line to the net and just sort of stared past me. It was kind of weird. Most people would be a bit self-conscious about looking in someone else's general direction, but not her. I could see her clearer now. Her hair was incredibly thick and shining and it hung down over her shoulders like it was the gentle waves of a black ocean. Her face was dark and her eyes, it appeared, were green. She was just wearing a white T-shirt and jeans, not the expensive kind, and had turned up her pants at the bottom, so you could see her bare calves. She had her hands on her hips and looked strong and fit. I was filled with a sensation that I hadn't had in a long time—maybe never. I wanted to talk to her. I was compelled to, believe it or not. I walked toward her. It seemed that she was a bit older than me, maybe seventeen, though it is hard to tell with girls. I got within about three or four metres.

"Hi," I said. I barely got it out. I wondered if it even sounded like "hi." Maybe it was more like a tiny bleat from a sheep, one whose voice was breaking.

She looked at me. It was as if she wasn't seeing me for a moment. Then I said something incredibly lame.

"I'm Dylan Maples."

I'm blaming him for that one, not me.

She kept staring at me, as if she were still gazing out over the water but had to look my way because I'd spoken. She didn't say anything for a while and I started to get really nervous.

"There's a storm coming," she finally said.

Then she walked away.

I WASN'T VERY INTERESTED in the beach after that. I felt like a total dolt. I wished I hadn't said anything. Girls want you to talk to them, don't they? But when you say something—

something nice, like "hi"—they just flip you off. I walked back to Bill and Bonnie's place, hoping they and the parental units had gone somewhere else, but they were in the living room, still talking. I could hear Bill's voice before I even got into the house. He still was going on about the young politician, saying once more how strange it felt for him to be leaning toward voting for a Conservative. Even an Independent one. I avoided them and went in the back way, straight up to my room, but it was awfully boring in there again. No phone.

I rolled around on the bed for a long while, and Mom came in to see me a couple of times and asked if I would like to join them in the living room.

"I know it is fascinating staring at the walls," she said, "but there are human beings in the house who may be almost as interesting."

I mumbled something about liking the view and was able to put her off twice, but knew it wouldn't work a third time. I heard a pause in the conversation downstairs and figured it was the moment to make a move, and a quick one. I could picture Mom getting up from her chair again and heading in my direction. I leapt to my feet, slipped from the bedroom and down the stairs, and out the back way. As I closed the door behind me, I heard a little commotion and noticed eight eyes staring at me from down the hallway. The dogs knew my secret. They didn't say a word, though.

It was getting dark outside and quieter. You could hear the waves crashing against the beach. Actually, they weren't crashing, just kind of washing in from the bay, sort of nice. The wind had picked up a little. I started to walk, heading east toward Youghall Beach where I had seen that girl.

There was no one around. No one except her.

I caught sight of her in the distance, standing on the beach near where I'd seen her before, looking out over the water again. I could just tell it was her. It was something in the way she stood, with her arms across her front, her feet set wide apart, almost as if in defiance of something or protecting herself. She had a way about her even from a great distance. I could see that long curly black hair hanging down her back. I kept walking toward her thinking that she would see me when I got to maybe within a hundred metres, since there was no one else on the beach, but I got within about fifty without her looking over. Then I was just twenty away and still no reaction, then I was close enough that I could talk to her in a normal voice, but I didn't say anything. Neither did she.

She kept staring out over the water. It was almost black now, or at least grey, with the sun having just set

over the horizon behind us. It was time for me to be
getting back but I couldn't move, and something inside
me was also telling me, maybe from all those lectures
that Dad had inflicted on me, that I shouldn't leave this
girl here all alone.

"Are you all right?" I finally asked.

She didn't respond for a moment and then turned
and looked at me. Her eyes seemed to shine, gazing out
from above her high cheekbones.

"Dylan Maples," she said.

Okay, I must be dreaming. This was another Alice. An
even better one. Here was this strange girl of Chaleur
Bay, like some sort of quiet goddess who had never
really acknowledged my existence and certainly never
addressed me, and the first thing she uttered was my
name. She said it beautifully and clearly. I had never
heard it said like that before. It made me feel proud,
which was something I hadn't felt for a while. It also
emboldened me to say something else.

"How do you know my name?"

"You told me."

"I know, but you weren't listening."

She smiled.

"You don't know a lot about girls, do you?"

She had an amazing way of talking, as if every word

were pronounced carefully and each one had a little on it, as they say in baseball, some sort of spirit attached to it, some sort of slight caress of the words. She had an accent. Not a big one, just a lilt. I could swear it was French, Quebecois, and yet it wasn't.

"I...I guess not," was all I could muster. A follow-up lame thing to say! I had to get something else out and fast. "What are you doing?"

"Nothing," she said.

I knew what she meant. Exactly what she meant. And it felt really cool.

"Not exactly nothing, though," I said.

She smiled. "No. I am looking. Searching."

That made a lot of sense too.

"Could you tell me your name?"

Man, what a rear end I am. Does anybody ever ask a question like that? And in that way? To a girl? An interesting one? It was like something the idiot says in a movie, the nerd, or just simply the guy that no girl in her right mind would give a second glance. Except to laugh at.

But she smiled again.

"Antonine," she said. "Antonine Marie Clay."

Wow. It was a magical name, said magically. I expected my alarm clock to go off at any second, Mom yelling at me to get up from downstairs in our house in Moore Park.

Instead, a ball of fire appeared out over the water.

Antonine turned her head as if a cannon had gone off. It was as though she had eyes, or ears, in the back of her head. I wondered how she could have spotted it. Perhaps the glow had entered her peripheral vision. I also wondered how she could see something that was obviously a figment of my imagination, for this was not a tiny spark like something made by a firefly—it was illuminating part of the bay way out there.

She stared at it and for a few seconds all I could do was look at her watching it, so intense was her attention. It was as if some force had turned her head and locked her vision onto this bizarre illusion of fire.

Then it started to move. It advanced across Chaleur Bay at the rate a sailboat would move. In fact, it even looked a little bit like one. A big, fiery sailboat. As I examined it, it appeared even more so. It made the soles of my feet tingle.

Then Antonine screamed, and it was bloodcurdling. I had never heard anyone do that. It was worse than anything a girl had to do in any movie. Antonine glanced at me in the middle of her scream and then began to run away into the darkness, off the beach, and out of sight. I could hear her footsteps pounding in the distance, even her heavy breathing, little shrieks coming from her, saying something that I couldn't understand. Something in some sort of French.

Then everything was silent, except for a whooshing sound, like a wind sound but more than that. It was like something *in* the wind. I turned back to the bay. The ball of fire was still there, moving faster now. And it looked even more like a ship! It seemed as though it was made of layers of flames piled high—a hull and sails above it. Something was definitely out there, on fire!

In seconds, however, it was gone, racing away in the opposite direction.

Then I was alone and scared. I actually ran back to Bill and Bonnie's place.

MOM WAS WAITING FOR me at the door. The back door.

"Found your escape route, Houdini," she said, "where were you?"

"Nowhere."

"Explanation, please."

"I was on the beach."

"It's dark out."

"Correct."

She sighed. "You do realize that it's dinnertime and

it's on the table waiting for us now. Waiting for you, to put it bluntly." Wow, I thought, I somehow hadn't been worrying about food. "You are going out there and apologizing. March."

I didn't have much choice and I can muster a pretty good apology face when I have to—kind of a looking-down-at-my-shoes kind of thing, soft voice, really sincere sounding. The Bill and Bonnie Show bought it, hook, line, and sinker.

Dinner wasn't much better for conversation than "late lunch." I found myself actually counting as I ate. One through ten, then one through fifty, then one through one hundred. It didn't help; the meal went on and on and on. The food was okay, some sort of fish ("local stuff," said Bill, "everything is local here, very important"), and tons more vegetables, all of them barely cooked, since that's what adults think is cool. Even the green beans were crunchy. Bonnie actually did a sort of "presentation" thing too, making every plate look like an art installation of food.

All a bit much, it seemed to me.

Bill was droning on again about his opinions and this young politician came up once more. He seemed obsessed with him, and kept apologizing for liking him, but definitely siding with him.

"He thinks our immigration levels are too high, and possibly he states his case a little too strongly sometimes. I'm all for bringing new folks into the country, but maybe the change should be a bit more gradual. We have such a lovely community here now, you know, the mixture of Acadians and the Indigenous people and English. I love it."

"Do you speak French?" I asked him. It just came right out of me. One of those "id" things again, I guess. I knew the answer.

"No," he said with a slightly forced smile, "but I'd like to."

Then get your butt in gear and learn, Mr. Bill, I felt like saying, but I really didn't want to pursue this— or anything else, to be honest—with this guy. I went back to counting. He pursued me a few times though, offering advice in that way that adults have, pretending they aren't offering advice at all. He complimented me on things in my personality that didn't really exist, like how hardworking he felt I likely was, and how different I was from other kids. Translation? "You need to work hard like I do, like my generation did, not like you lazy dirtbags do, and you had better not be anything like the rest of your lot or you aren't going anywhere in life."

"I definitely believe in change," said Bill at the head of the table, "I'm a new-ways kind of guy, always been about that, but sometimes the old ways are the better ways."

Spoken like an old guy, I thought.

Thank God that one didn't come shooting out of my mouth.

I hung in there for a long time, well after we had finished the fruit bowl of dessert. I even gave my confinement a few more beats after that before I asked to be excused in an incredibly polite voice.

"I'm awfully tired. I think I'll turn in for the night," I said.

Turn in struck me as a suitably outdated phrase for the Bill and Bonnie Show. I thought they might appreciate it. Mom gave me a bit of a look, but then smiled when Bonnie commented on my manners and let me go.

As I passed the big picture window, I looked out and saw the slate-dark sea. I could hear the wind and the waves.

"Folks around here say that's the way the water looks the day before a storm," I heard Bonnie say behind me.

5

THE LEGEND

"I'm going to go down to the beach, Mom, is that okay? It really is nice down there."

We had just finished breakfast of granola and yogurt. I think Mom was hoping that I would hang out with her, Dad, and our hosts for a while. She started to open her mouth to say no.

"Of course," said Bonnie.

Compliment the hosts on their beach and get what you want. Nice move, Dylan Maples.

At least he was good for something.

"Uh, not for long, and don't stray too far. Don't go deep-sea diving or anything," said Mom, "We are all heading out for a drive in about an hour." She looked out the big picture window. "It actually doesn't seem like such a great day for the beach anyway."

She was right. It wasn't raining or anything, or even cold, it was just kind of grey and there was a breeze blowing in from the water, as if it was announcing that something was on the way. The beach wasn't very crowded, just the odd old couple out for a walk.

I headed for Youghall.

She was there again, but this time she seemed different. She wasn't staring out at the sea. She was walking along it toward me, really toward me this time.

"Hi," she said.

"Hi," I replied cleverly.

"No school today, one of those professional development days for the teachers, so I came here, hoping you would show up."

Really? You did? At least, I felt like saying that. My heart started thumping. I couldn't talk.

"I owe you an explanation," she said, filling in the silence.

"Oh, you mean for the blood-curdling shriek and the sprint in the opposite direction?" Somehow I got that out, despite the fact that I was breathing heavily and hoping it didn't show.

She laughed. That was an amazing start. Given that I was useless around girls these days, and that this one was a bit older than me and incredibly interesting, I felt like I was some sort of male god when she did that. Well, as male god as it is possible for me to think of myself being, which isn't very male god.

"Let's sit down," she said. We walked over to a log and sat together. My right leg was about a metre from hers, maybe about three-quarters of a metre, perhaps seventy centimetres. She had jeans on again and a different T-shirt. Now she seemed like she was about twenty-one or something, but I knew that wasn't true. My leg, next to hers, appeared awfully scrawny, even though it was longer. Her leg looked kind of soft and smooth, right through the pant leg.

"I turned sixteen a while ago," she said, almost as if she had read my mind.

You look like it, and more, I wanted to say, and then lay a lie on her, tell her I was sixteen too, even though that birthday was still a couple of months away for me.

She kept talking, thank God. I didn't want her to guess my age, since she might figure I was about twelve...a five foot, eight inch twelve year old with pontoons for feet.

"So, don't go thinking I'm just a scared little kid when I tell you this."

"I would never think that," I said and then wondered if that was the right thing to say, but she smiled at it too. *Yes!* Going well so far.

"I was upset last night. Not just because of what we saw, but because of what it means to me."

I glanced toward the bay. "What *did* we see?"

She laughed again. I had the feeling that she wasn't a laugher. It struck me that she was a serious sort and rather smart. She just had that way about her. So, making her laugh was probably a good thing. It might even mean that I was impressing her. I'd seen lots of headlines in women's magazines about female celebrities saying that what they wanted in a guy was "a sense of humour." That seemed a bit weird to me. Didn't looks come first or at least a pretty close second? Wasn't that the truth? Or was that really shallow? I wasn't sure if Antonine interested me because of her appearance or what. I just knew I wanted to be near her.

"We saw the ghost ship."

"Pardon me?"

"It was amazing," she continued, as if I hadn't said anything. "We saw the burning ghost ship of Chaleur

Bay. It is famous. Many people have seen it. I saw it one other time, long ago." She stopped for a second, looked very serious, and stared out over the water. "It freaked me out yesterday not just because it appeared, which is bad enough, but because I had this weird feeling I was going to see it last night. That is why I was down at the water in the first place. It isn't the sort of thing you should be able to predict, though. I knew the skies and the wind were changing and that people say it sometimes comes in that sort of weather."

Okay, I thought, *I have met the girl from my dreams and she is insane.*

"It wasn't a ghost ship," I said.

That was a mistake. She turned and glared at me. Her green eyes lit up. It was kind of cool, actually, she looked amazing, but I knew I'd stepped in it.

"You're a jerk," she said.

"I know," I said immediately. Another "id" thing, but at least it was honest. She had basically said what I was thinking, what I had been thinking for a year or so now. It had a strange effect on her, though. It softened her eyes immediately.

"Sorry," she said.

"No, no, I'm sorry."

"That's awfully Canadian of you, Dylan, but let me talk."

"Okay."

"I understand that it's a bit much to swallow when someone just up and starts talking about seeing a ghost. I get it, and to be honest, I am not really saying that it was definitely that. What we saw might have been some sort of natural phenomenon."

"What?"

"That's what some people say it is."

"I saw a ball of fire out on the water. At least, I think I did. Is that what you saw?"

"Didn't it seem like more than that?"

"No," I lied.

"The thing about a ghost, Dylan, is that usually just one person sees it, and then either keeps quiet about it or tries to convince others it exists. Two of us saw that thing last night and in the past there have often been more than two witnesses at a time."

There was silence for a moment.

"Tell me what you mean by 'natural phenomenon.'"

"Uh, some people—researchers and scientists— who can't deny that people have seen fire out on the bay here moving across it like a ship, say it has to be caused by something in the water or a weird effect of the light out there. Apparently, some of these experts say it might be phosphorescence in the water, whatever that is. Others have theorized it might be something called St. Elmo's fire, which is a real thing, a natural phenomenon, but it has to do with lightning striking some sort of high surface, like a tower or a building, which there obviously are none of out on the bay. And there was no lightning last night anyway." She paused, and looked at me. "People study this thing, Dylan, and yet everyone seems to have a different explanation. It hasn't been seen very often, maybe every few years or so people report it, but don't you think it's freaky that more than one person can see it at once? Crowds of people have actually observed it."

"Crowds?" I was thinking of taking back my theory that nothing weird happens in New Brunswick.

"Yes. More than once."

"Really?"

"And it's pretty freaky, too, that you and I saw it, just happened to, the first time I met you."

There was silence again.

"So, what are you saying? If there are so many explanations, which one is right?"

"What I said: it's a ship from the past, on fire."

I didn't say anything. I thought that was wisest.

"At least...that's what people say. Think about it again and tell me the truth: did it look at all like that to you?"

I couldn't actually remember now, not clearly anyway. It had sort of messed with my mind, and I realized I had convinced myself it wasn't real, that I had simply seen a light on the water and I may have even made that up. That's how much Antonine's reaction had freaked me out. There had to have been some sort of illumination out there, though. Or I was crazy...or she was. I focused on the memory and could see the object again. It had certainly looked like it was sailing over the water. I didn't want to concentrate on it for long. It was just too weird.

"I don't know," I finally said.

"Well, many witnesses recount all sorts of details about it, and the burning ships they describe are always very old; vessels with masts from hundreds of years ago, like explorers' crafts or pirate ships."

Okay, so now we were talking about pirates. And, uh, not just pirates, but pirates on ships from eons ago. Ghosts, on fire, sailing across Chaleur Bay in plain sight...in the twenty-first century.

"There are lots of different legends about it," said Antonine. She looked back out over the water. "Some say the ship is Portuguese, others say Spanish or French or English. They can tell by the masts, the design of the ship. One story is that the whole thing has to do with a real sixteenth-century sailor who was brutally murdered by the locals and is now haunting the waters here. Lots of stories say the ship is connected to the Indigenous people from the area, the Mi'kmaq, and that some of their young women were attacked by Europeans, abused and killed, and that you can see one of those women at the helm of the ship, hanging out over it as it sails through the bay."

"Wow." Not very articulate, but it pretty accurately described what I was feeling.

Then I had the sense that I should put my arm around her or something, because her eyes were filling with tears. What was that all about? Why would an old story, a legend, regardless of how creepy it was, make her cry? Maybe girls just cried at stuff like this? But I didn't think so. This really meant something to her.

"I came out here yesterday to try to see it," Antonine stifled a sob. "And it appeared. I…I can't believe it."

"But—"

"This is the time of year people always see it," she continued. "And the conditions will be perfect once more: a northeast wind, a storm that moves in slowly, a temperature that generates a wisp of fog…absolutely perfect…tonight." She wasn't looking at me.

"Are you coming back tonight?" I asked.

"They say that if two people see it together more than once," she added in a distant voice, "that their fates are entwined forever."

Wow. I didn't say it out loud this time though, just thought it. I looked out over the water too, kind of turned away from her now.

I tried harder to remember exactly what that fire had looked like yesterday. How does fire ignite on water? How does it move across the surface? I just couldn't bring it back clearly, though. All I could remember was a vague image, and Antonine. She was kind of blocking my memory.

"I remember meeting you better than seeing the ship," I admitted. I couldn't believe I actually let that one slip out. What a bonehead thing to say.

She didn't respond. She didn't say anything for the longest time and I couldn't bring myself to look at her. If she was glaring at me, that wouldn't be good, but if she was smiling it might not be good either. What would I do? I kept wondering about her tears too, and her scream. Why such an extreme reaction? Finally, I mustered up the courage to turn and look at her.

I was all alone on Youghall Beach on Chaleur Bay.

6

ACADIA

Mom was more than a touch angry and it was hard to blame her. I had promised I wouldn't be gone for long but apparently I had been out on the beach for nearly two hours. It certainly hadn't felt like it. She was charging along the sand toward me when I first caught a glimpse of her. There weren't too many others around and I spotted her pretty quickly. She was the only one glaring at me.

"What are you trying to pull, young man?" was her first question. I'm never really sure what that means—literally.

"I'm coming," I said, making toward her as fast as I could go.

The "coming" thing again. Not nearly as effective, though, when they can see you. That was when she explained about the two hours and saw my amazed reaction.

"That's twice you've done this now! What is the big attraction on the beach? What could you possibly have been doing out here for two hours? Alone?"

Good question.

"I'm looking forward to the drive." It was the only thing I could think of saying. It was a long shot. And it didn't work.

"Oh, give me a break. Come on!"

THE BILL AND BONNIE Show made its way onto the road around Bathurst late that morning. Bonnie had packed a lunch. More quinoa and veggies. We went everywhere, it seemed. First, they drove along their road, Queen Elizabeth Drive, noting some of the nicer homes and commenting on the people who lived there in complimentary ways. It seemed like everyone they knew was from Ontario. Then they took us to Youghall Beach. We drove in and left Bill's SUV in the sandy parking lot and walked around a bit, past the volleyball games and out onto the beach. I pretended that I hadn't been in this area before. I was really hoping that Antonine wasn't around, and it seemed that she wasn't. Maybe this wasn't her scene; she was more into early mornings and stormy nights.

Then we drove into Bathurst, and got out on Queen Street for a stroll.

"Let's go in here," said Bonnie to Mom as we approached a women's clothing store, "they have some great summer stuff."

That left Bill, Dad, and me standing on the street. Soon, we were sitting on a bench.

"Lovely day," said Bill.

"Marvelous," replied Dad.

That was about as exciting as it got.

Driving along Harbourfront Boulevard looking out at the water was only marginally better. Once we were through town, out on the east side along the shore, we stopped at a place called Salmon Beach. We bought some snacks—if you can call them that, not a chip, Twizzler, or Skittle among the goodies—lots of "real food" things masquerading as cookies and candies; even the brownies didn't have any sugar in them. The labels were like billboards advertising how incredibly healthy they were and how intelligent you were for choosing to eat such nutritious food.

Then it was back into Bill's vehicle and through some villages in that area. I had to admit it was impressive.

The houses weren't as fancy as Bill and Bonnie's but they were certainly rustic—*actually* rustic—mostly wooden homes, spaced a good distance from each other along the road, many facing out toward the beautiful blue water. Everything on land was very green, with amazing stretches of trees and fields. Things got more French too, many of the restaurants, little businesses, and churches and arenas had French names. "Acadian," I suppose, was the accurate term, which is what the French Canadians from around here call themselves.

"This is Grande-Anse," said Bill as we passed through one particularly nice village. He tried to pronounce it in French, though what he came up with sounded more like "grand ass." He pointed forward, like a captain in charge of a ship. "Soon we will be in Caraquet; so picturesque and wonderfully Acadian, it's the heart of our area. There's a story or two I'd like to share with you about these parts...." And he launched into the first one, a real snore-fest.

It was a bit of a relief when we stopped at this pioneer place called Village historique acadien and he had to shut up for a while so the real experts could talk about the history of the area. I am funny about history. I actually like it and do very well in school in the subject. I think it is because history is like a story to me. During

every family trip we have gone on, I've learned some
amazing things about other places. I sometimes think
there is a sort of prejudice against the past. Many people
don't like it because it is gone, it's just old peoples'
stories, and even though they're invisible now, we
really judge them for the morals they had. But we will
be judged too...or forgotten.

This Acadian village was very cool. First of all, it
was frighteningly bilingual. I'm working on my French
in school, but all of the village's employees (who were
dressed up in period costumes, even the kids), could
speak French or English at the drop of a hat. They
switched back and forth, sometimes mid-sentence. It
made me kind of jealous.

"Bonjour, hello," said the young woman who greeted
us just inside the entrance.

"English, please," said Bonnie pleasantly.

"Absolument! You are now about to go back in time!"

The first place we went to was an Acadian pioneer
home. We climbed some steps into an old wooden
cabin. There was a guy there in stockings that came up
to the knees of his pants and he was wearing a wide
straw hat.

"Bonjour, hello," he said.

"English," commanded Bill.

We were in what likely would have passed for a living and dining area, but it was really just a small room with a pot-belly stove. There was a model of a ship on a table and some drawings of other ships beside it. They were obviously images of the ships the Europeans sailed when they first came here—Portuguese and Spanish fishing boats, French and English war vessels. It made me think of Antonine and the ghost ship.

We toured old hotels, stores, and little barns and sheds, and saw how people in those days made straw brooms and baked bread.

"Tell me about the earliest Acadian days," said Dad to one the hosts in the barn. She was wearing a long thick dress that went all the way down to the floor and a bonnet that looked like it might have kept the sun off but would be hot too. She had just risen from milking a cow.

"I don't think that's her department. She wouldn't know much about—" began Bonnie.

"Well, they first came here from France in the early 1600s," said the woman, kind of ignoring Bonnie, "and had basically set up a country in the area called Acadia or Acadie. Just like the hockey team!"

She smiled at me. I smiled back, making sure Bill and Bonnie saw it, too.

"Once the British started winning the never-ending war for North America with the French, though, including that incredible battle at the Plains of Abraham in Quebec City, the Acadians were on the wrong side," she continued. "The British wanted them to pledge allegiance but they were people with lots of integrity and wouldn't do it." She looked proud when she said that. "So...the British kicked them out! They forced them to leave." Now she looked a little angry. "The Acadians left in many thousands, some right into the woods to hide, and we know New Brunswick has lots of trees!"

She laughed out loud, and Mom, Dad, and I laughed with her.

"Some went over to Europe, too, and many of them down to the States to Louisiana where they became the Cajun people. However, many of them came back, and started building villages like the one you are exploring today."

She paused for a second and her eyes got a little misty.

"There is a famous poem about it all called *Évangéline* by an American writer named Henry Wadsworth Longfellow. It's about two young lovers who got separated during "Le Grand Dérangement" and finally find each other in old age when she discovers him dying in a hospital in the US. It's really, really sad."

The woman looked a bit emotional, despite the fact that she must have told this story hundreds of times before. She turned back to the cow. I know some girls in school who might tear up over that one, too.

Acadian culture was interesting and it was still vibrant. We learned that Acadians have their own flag, their own music, language, all that kind of thing. We heard some of their songs when we were there: two old guys playing violins—or fiddles, I guess— and other guys dancing to it. Yes: guys. It was neat, though.

There was a place near the exit where they made all sorts of Acadian food, so we got to eat some—fish cakes and some of that freshly baked bread. Awesome stuff. I asked for seconds, and could have had thirds, fourths, and fifths...and maybe beyond.

There was a bit of a commotion on a bridle path about fifty metres from us as we were leaving.

"Hey," said Bill, "it's Jim Fiat. He must have been moving around in the village while we were inside."

It was the Independent candidate in the election, here to shake hands.

"Let's go over and say hello."

"Uh...why don't just you two go," said Mom. "We'll wait for you."

Mom and Dad leaned against a rail fence, but the politician was moving on an angle that was leading him somewhat in our direction, so by the time Bill and Bonnie got to him, he wasn't too far away. Bonnie hung back a little but Bill stepped right up and took Fiat's meaty hand, instantly extended toward him. I took a few steps forward and watched.

The candidate was a squarely built man with perfectly combed blond hair and a mega-watt smile, wearing an open-collar white shirt meant to look casual but perfectly tailored and actually shining in the sun. I could see a gold chain around his neck. He and Bill chatted for a while. Fiat whispered in Bill's ear at one point while gripping his arm and shared a laugh, then embraced him before they parted.

Once we were all back in the car, we headed out toward the highway to turn down to Caraquet and started talking about what we had seen. Though we had to have a report on Jim Fiat first.

"He seemed like a very nice man," said Bonnie, "I was a bit surprised."

"Great guy," said Bill, "looked me right in the eye. He just blended into the crowd like an average person."

"That's nice," said Dad, who seemed anxious to change the subject. "I thought the village was marvellous."

"Yes, but as Jim Fiat pointed out to me, it would be nice if it were completely authentic." Bonnie was handing him his driving glasses, his third pair.

"What do you mean?" asked Dad. "I felt like I was back in time."

"Jim noticed a girl wearing a hijab, making cheese in one of the stables. That wouldn't have been the case back in those days, clothes-wise. Jim said he had a nice chat with her, though. She's from the Middle East."

"I didn't notice the hijab," said Dad. "I think it's more the spirit of the thing that matters."

Sometimes, like right at that moment, I am a big fan of John Maples.

Soon, Bill launched into more of his theories about everything under the sun. I had actually really enjoyed the historic village...and now I had to listen to him drone on again. I let my mind drift back to Antonine. It occurred to me that she was probably Acadian, with that amazing French-and-English name of hers and that slight lilt in the way she talked. Man, she was amazing. I just kept thinking about her. I wished she wasn't so fixated on that so-called ghost ship, though. That worried me. I mean, I had seen it too, but I doubted it was anything more than some sort of weird light on the water.

"Have you ever heard of the burning ghost ship of Chaleur Bay?" I suddenly blurted out, stopping Bill mid-lecture.

There was a pause.

"Yes," he said, "as a matter of fact I have."

"Have you ever seen it?"

He laughed. "Dylan, what a question! It's just a local legend. I don't believe in ghosts. No one in his or her right mind does. I know this thing has supposedly been seen by a whole bunch of people at once, but consider the people—" He stopped the instant he said that.

"You don't really mean it that way, dear, I know," said Bonnie quickly.

"Of course I don't! I love the people around here. But it is a crazy story. A folk tale."

Okay, now I wanted to believe Antonine completely. "Consider the people!" What an ignorant thing to say. I wouldn't trade a thousand Mr. Bills for Antonine.

"I have a friend who has a friend who was in a group that saw it," said Bonnie, kind of quietly. "It was quite a sight, the way she told it."

"Mass hallucination," said Bill.

CARAQUET WAS VERY NICE, picturesque indeed, with lots of wood-frame homes; very green, too, and it seemed every store, church, and sign was French. We were truly in the heart of Acadia. There were even Acadian flags hanging on the street posts: red, white, and blue like the France flag, but with a little yellow star in the upper left corner.

"This is the capital of Acadia," said Bill. "You just missed National Acadian Day last month. The folks around here really do it up right. They have this thing called 'tintamarre' where they all dress up in their colours and make lots of noise and parade around and sing their national anthem, *Ave Maris Stella*, it's fabulous."

I doubted that he pronounced the title of the Acadian national anthem correctly. It sounded like an old white man from Toronto trying to say a few words in Swahili or something. I didn't like the way he talked about Acadians, period. It was as if he thought they were cute or something. One of them is, I know that for certain, but she isn't cute in the way he meant it. His tone, to me, was kind of condescending.

I couldn't wait to get back to Bill and Bonnie's house, and not because I wanted to hang out. I was planning another trip to the beach, a late-night one. I was pretty sure Antonine was going to be there again. I remembered what she said about the ghost ship appearing in a certain sort of weather.

The wind was picking up, coming from the north.

7

NIGHTTIME ESCAPE

I had to give Mom and Dad the slip again. Well, really just Mom. The word Mom used for Dad sometimes was "oblivious" and it was pretty accurate, though I must admit I'm kind of like that too. Mom seems to be able to focus on about sixteen things at once, but Dad doesn't really have that ability. He was having a holiday with his friends, so that was what was on his mind. I get it. When I'm focused on something, there is nothing else going on in the world. And I was making plans about the beach, the fire on the water…and Antonine.

Mom, however, was watching me like a hawk. It's funny with her. It's like I'm always playing a sort of cat-and-mouse game with old Laura. She is just so aware of

me all the time, worried about me, providing for me...
not always giving me space. It's like she is in my head
at times. Well, not literally in my head, just trying to
get in. She also knew that I knew that she was like that.
So today, with her current worries about me and her
already catching me spending so long at the beach, I
really had to be on top of my game if I was going to give
her the slip.

No one was hungry due to the snacks and the meal
we had at the historic village, so we were going to have
"late dinner." We wouldn't eat until it was dark out. I
spent a little bit of time talking with the adults when we
got back. I made sure I participated in the conversation
this time, tried to be ridiculously polite, and even did
my best to agree with Bill's sucky opinions. It was part
of my strategy. I was hoping it would let Mom's defenses
down a little, not make her so hyper-aware of me and my
movements.

The weather was getting worse; you could hear the
wind blowing and the waves now actually crashing
against the shore.

"Definite storm on the way," observed Bonnie.

I didn't ask to be excused until a good hour into the
conversation. The sun was getting low on the far side
of the house, casting this weird glow over the water.

Given the impeccable manners and interest in adult concerns I had been showing, everyone was more than pleased to let me leave the table when I finally asked. I headed for my room.

Mom positioned herself in a chair so she had a view down the hall, right toward the back door I would have to use to get out of the house. Man, she was good.

When I got to my room, I didn't lay on the bed. I stood near the door and listened to the conversation. I let it go on for a while, dying to sneak downstairs, peek around the corner, and down the hall toward Mom. I didn't dare, though. If she spotted me, that would end my plans. So I just listened for the right moment.

Finally, it came.

"Laura," said Bonnie, "take a look at this plant. The blooms are amazing. Perennial, with lots of details in the colours."

I heard Mom respond and her voice move across the room.

Time for action.

I opened my door, eased downstairs, glanced along the hall toward Mom's now-empty chair, slipped into open view and noticed that Dad was now visible, his face pointed directly toward me as he chatted away to Bill. My heart sank. Then I realized that he wasn't even noticing me. I even waved my hands in the air to see if that got any reaction.

Nothing.

"Government should be run like a business," said Bill, "that's my view."

"Really?" said Dad. "But government isn't simply about money and profit, is it? Isn't it more about doing the right thing, supporting people, not just the bottom line? That can be inhuman."

"Well, it has to be efficient. This Jim Fiat guy, he understands that."

"I have to say, Bill, I have my doubts about him."

I wanted to hear more of Dad disagreeing with Bill, but I had to get away. I had to be *efficient*. I glanced at the four dogs, who had padded into the hallway and were staring at me again, tongues hanging out and tails wagging. I turned to the outside door, opened it, and then closed it behind me as I escaped without a sound.

It was such an amazing sense of freedom to be outside. The wind had definitely picked up and I was actually a little cold in my Leafs T-shirt and jeans. I made my way around to the beach side and crouched down below the ridge of long grass that ran between the house and the sand until I was sure I was out of the sightline Mom might have through the picture window. Then I started to run toward Youghall Beach.

Last night, there had been a few couples walking along the water holding hands, but tonight there was no one around. I guess everyone knew a storm was coming; maybe they could sense how strange it was for the wind to blow from this direction and maybe the fog spooked them, too. It all made me even more certain that Antonine would be at Youghall.

I saw her from a long way off, looking like she was a sort of mythic figure of a girl, a sweatshirt on this time, red, white, and blue, with ACADIA written across the front in big letters. She was hugging herself in the cool wind, but staring right into it, her long black hair blowing around. I just stopped and looked at her for a while.

She didn't acknowledge my presence for the longest time, even when I walked right up to her. I had never been this close. I was less than an arm's length away. Her face was in profile, her skin looking incredibly smooth, her chin stuck out a little, as if anticipating something.

"Hi," she said.

"Come here often?" I replied. Wow, that was maybe the lamest thing I had said to her, and I had said some ridiculous stuff. But she smiled, thank God.

"Actually," she said, "I'll probably be here tomorrow, if you're interested, at least in the morning. Half of the school is going on a field trip, but not me. So, I have the morning off. A day and a half in a row away from school. Not bad."

I knew what she meant, but I was more into the fact that she was basically inviting me to see her again. That was hard to believe, though. How could *this* girl want to see *me* again? I wanted to keep her interested in me. I had read somewhere that what girls really like is when you ask them about things that deeply matter to them.

"Hey, why did you scream? You didn't tell me why, really."

She didn't say anything, so neither did I. We just stood there, looking out over the water. I actually was peeking at her for part of it, just moving my eyeballs, catching sideways glances.

And then it returned.

She put her hand to her lips and let out a little cry.

A red ball of fire, way out on Chaleur Bay.

"I don't think it has ever appeared two days in a row," she whispered.

Then she started to run. At first, I thought she was trying to get away again.

"Antonine!" I cried. "It's okay, it's just a weird light! Stay with me! We'll watch it, you'll see!"

She, however, had turned and rushed directly away from the beach. For an instant, I didn't go after her. I looked back out toward the water. And I just about fainted. It wasn't simply a ball of fire. There was no way it was only that. It was moving again, a huge flame maybe a kilometre away, pulsing as if the wind were inside it, a more distinct and solid mass at the bottom like the hull this time, billowing lighter flames at the top like sails. Figures seemed to be moving around in it now and something at the front, another figure, this one writhing, appeared to be tied to what looked like a mast. The ship was almost lighting up the horizon!

I turned and ran. I would like to say it was because I wanted to protect Antonine, and comfort her, but I was scared. Big time.

Then I had the sense that someone was watching me from behind. He had just materialized on the beach.

Bomber.

"Don't follow her—not tonight!" he cried. "Stay with me!"

I left him behind.

I could see Antonine in the dim light, about a hundred metres away by now, not turning at the road that leads off the beach, but running right across it, toward the water on the other side. Youghall Beach was a sort of peninsula, with an access road, trees and parking areas in the middle and whatever on the other side. I had no idea what was there. Likely just more beach. By the time I reached the road, however, I could tell it was more than that. Antonine had gone through a wide gate in a fence and I could see she was heading toward a building near the water. I ran harder. She could really move.

The building, pale blue or grey with a sharply peaked roof, had writing on it: BATHURST MARINA.

"Antonine!" I cried.

She turned around when she heard me and I saw a look of fear on her face.

"Go, Dylan! Go away!"

She was making for the marina's boats, moored in two long docks that went out into the water from a small hook-shaped peninsula of sand and rocks. Antonine hit one of the docks on the fly and started looking at each boat as she went past it, her head darting from one to the next. I followed her.

"Antonine!" I yelled again once I felt the dock wobble beneath my feet. "What are you doing?"

"Go home!" she yelled back, without even looking my way. "Go away!"

I wasn't about to do that. I tried walking along the dock. I'm definitely a city guy, hardly ever been in a boat in my life. A few times in Newfoundland, and the last time in Harrison Lake at Harrison Hot Springs near Sasquatch Provincial Park in BC...where the made-up Alice lives.

Alice—I mean Antonine—stopped near a boat and jumped right into it. I couldn't believe it. It was a motorboat of some sort. She bent under the steering wheel and started doing something down there. I approached and stood on the dock right near her.

"What are you doing?"

I could see that her hands were shaking.

"Go away," she repeated. "This doesn't concern you."

I heard the motor roar. Somehow, she'd jigged it.

"Undo those!" she yelled, pointing at the ropes that tied the boat to the dock.

"What? Is this your boat? It's dark out!"

She jumped up and undid the ropes herself, then kicked the dock to push the boat away from it. The boat floated out into the water and she got into position behind the steering wheel. Then I did something really stupid.

I leapt into the boat.

8

THE BURNING GHOST SHIP

Antonine confirmed my opinion.

"That was really stupid!" she cried, but she wasn't even looking at me, or offering to set me back on land. She was pushing the throttle down and roaring out of the marina, turning a sharp left as she hit the more open water in the cove and heading straight out toward Chaleur Bay and the endless horizon.

Well, not just the horizon—she was moving directly toward the ball of fire.

That, believe it or not, wasn't our biggest problem. The waves were getting higher by the minute and the boat—which seemed to me wasn't fit for being out in a night like this—was climbing them, one after the other, then

86

smashing down. Climbing, smashing down, climbing, smashing down. It felt like a deadly rhythm. I was lying on the bottom of the boat at the back, clinging to a seat, getting soaked, and praying. I'm not a praying person. It seemed, however, at that moment, like the appropriate thing to do. That, and crying. But I was too scared to cry.

I kept staring at the back of Antonine's head. She looked powerful from behind with her long black curly hair flying out behind her as if she were some sort of modern-day Medusa taking me to hell. She was gripping the wheel hard and just going with the pounding we were taking, standing up as she drove, rising a little onto the balls of her feet as we ascended each wave, and taking the impact with her knees in a wide stance as we dropped down. Her eyes seemed to be locked onto the fire out in front of her, almost as if she had forgotten I was even there. She was hunting this phantom. It seemed like she wanted to drive right into it!

I tried to call out to her but I couldn't find my voice and it was so loud now that she likely couldn't have heard me if I'd screamed anyway.

We drew closer and closer, somehow staying afloat, though it felt like the waves were getting even higher and that with one descent and a cross wind, we would hit the water sideways, capsize, and die under the stormy surface of Chaleur Bay. I imagined flying out of the boat, maybe landing on the motor, my body ripped apart, blood splattering everywhere. I'm a bit like that in the imagination department.

I started thinking of Mom and Dad too, mostly Mom, wanting me to stay in the house. They were likely about to start dinner, Mom finding me absent, angry with me, not knowing I was about to die. She would regret her anger later. They always do.

The fire was nearing, and Antonine was still driving directly at it. She had seemed so intriguing to me, and yet now she would be the cause of my death. I wondered if that was a sort of thing in life; that the things you love and that fascinate you are also the things that can destroy you.

Then something even worse happened.

We were about a couple hundred metres from the fire and we hit a monster wave. It was like a mountain, and when we came down its other side, it knocked Antonine backwards. She came flying toward me, straight back, and smacked her head on the aluminum bench in front of me.

She lay there, motionless.

"Antonine!" I cried. I pulled her up onto my

lap. Stilled by the nature she was a part of, she was mesmerizing as she lay in my arms. I had no time to pause, though. The boat didn't have a pilot.

I was not a good candidate for the job. Not a good one at all. The worst, in fact. I figured if I had walked along the beach when it was packed or even gone into Bathurst and knocked on every door, I wouldn't have been able to find a worse candidate. A small child would have been better.

But I had no choice. The boat was turning sideways. The next wave was approaching. The big fire in front of me didn't concern me one bit now. It was as if it had become just a minor player in all of this.

I somehow shot forward and reached for the controls. My feet went out from under me and my face hit the steering wheel with a crack.

Everything went dark for a second, then it was blurry, and then it cleared. I gripped the wheel.

Back home, Dad often let me operate the ride-on lawn mower. It was a bit of a joke that we even owned one, since our lawn was postage-stamp size, but I liked to roar around on the thing, pushing the throttle down, taking corners way tighter than I needed to, imagining I was at the Indy 500 or something. That was the extent of my steering experience.

I wanted to immediately turn the boat around but something told me I shouldn't steer sideways into the waves, that such a move would just tip us, so I kept going forward, toward the ball of fire. It was lighting up everything around us now, a monster about to engulf us. This was a Guillermo del Toro movie I did not want to see. I stared at it as we crested the wave. What I saw freaked me out.

It was a ship. There was no doubt. A burning ship!

The masts were billowing in the wind and there were balls of flames underneath those flames that looked like the heads of crew members and a larger one, full-bodied, like a captain near the helm, his hands on something like a steering wheel. Then I saw another form, white-hot and shimmering, wearing a dress or smock of some sort, writhing, her flesh on fire, strapped to the bow of the ship, leading it forward. She was screaming.

I stared at it all, open-mouthed, no concern for my safety anymore, entranced by the fiery phantom ship of Chaleur Bay.

Then we struck the bottom of a wave and I came to my senses with a thump. I turned our little motorboat in a tight maneuver, like Shaun White on the side of a giant half-pipe. I didn't care anymore about being a bad driver attempting a difficult turn—we had to get away from here or we'd die anyway. We shot up the wave and landed on the other side. Somehow, the boat was pointed the opposite direction, back toward the shore and Youghall Beach. I pulled back the throttle and we roared off.

"Where is it?" I heard a woozy voice say. I looked back to see Antonine rising to her feet, somehow steady in the rocky boat.

"Stay down," I shouted, "you hit your head."

She didn't pay any attention. Instead, she advanced toward me, scanning the horizon. Then, realizing which direction we were going, seized the wheel from me and whipped our vessel sideways, doing a 180 and catching air. I fell back to the bottom of the boat, but somehow scrambled back up onto shaky legs.

We were going back out toward the open bay!

Then she slowed the boat. Our fire was gone. The stormy horizon was dark, grey, and empty.

"Where did it go?" cried Antonine.

It had sailed away, out of sight; or perhaps it had sunk; or it had never been there in the first place.

"It's gone!" she shouted.

"It was a just a light!" I cried. "Just a light on the water. We have to get back to shore!"

I didn't really believe that, though.

All along the return trip, clutching the side of the boat and wanting to clutch Antonine, I kept thinking about what I had seen. I remembered striking my head on the steering wheel. I had hallucinated, seen a vision, nothing more. That must be it, I told myself.

I STAGGERED OFF THE dock and onto the sand, got onto all fours, and threw up. I really hated that in about a thousand different ways. Firstly, it was gross, secondly it made me look like a wuss, and lastly Antonine had to witness it. She was awesome about it, though. She actually knelt beside me and put her hand on my back as I retched, comforting me. This from someone who had been knocked silly just fifteen minutes or so before.

Once I got to my feet, it got even better.

"I'm going to have to hug you," she said.

"Uh...."

"To keep you warm."

Then she took me into her arms. I cannot describe how that felt. I absolutely cannot describe it. The best attempt might be to say that she felt soft and strong at the same time, and that I somehow seemed quite warm as I shivered in her embrace. The wind whipped around us, sometimes even pushing us closer together.

"I'm going to tell you why I screamed," she said, her

head slightly below mine, her voice a bit muffled. She pressed her mouth into my shoulder.

"My father's name was Jackson Clay and he wasn't from here. He came to this area from the United States about twenty years ago and met my mother, who is Acadian. He hadn't intended to stay. He was from Alabama, a teacher, very interested in history and culture, well aware that he had Acadian roots on his mother's side. My Mom worked for the Bathurst Public Library. He stopped by to ask some questions and do some research, saw her, talked to her, and never left."

That was kind of the way I was feeling about Antonine right now. I planned to never leave her. She smelled good. How was that even possible when you have just been out in a storm?

"My father was African American. He gave up his life in the States to live here with Mom. She just never could have left."

Was. She kept saying, "was," about him. That was not a good sign.

"They got married and eventually had me. I'm an only child."

Like me, I thought.

"Things didn't go well for them. I don't mean in their marriage, that was great. I never saw two people more in love than my Mom and Dad. It was as if they were physically attached to each other half the time. They were always holding hands and hugging. Other things about their getting together, however, were not so great. He had a hard time finding a job. He had to take all sorts of courses to be qualified to teach here and he ended up mostly being a part-time teacher. His income combined with Mom's as a part-time librarian didn't amount to much. We really struggled."

Her voice faded a bit when she said that.

"It's okay," I said. Man, what a bone-headed thing to say! What did I even mean by that? It just came out. She gave me a little squeeze, though.

"Are you any warmer?" she asked.

I wanted to say no, so she would keep holding on to me, but I had to be honest, I was getting warm. Really warm actually, even though I was just in my T-shirt. It didn't seem right for us to be hugging like that.

"I'm all right now," I said.

She pulled back from me and started walking up the path toward the main road that led into Youghall. She rubbed her head and neck a bit, and started talking again, in a low voice, so I hustled to catch up to her and hear what she was saying.

"We lived in a little house in Bathurst, still do. Mom and Dad always emphasized education and really pushed me, and I felt a responsibility to work hard. I have had the best marks in every class I have been in since I started school. I always wanted to go to university and knew I had to have scholarships to do be able to afford that. I do not want to brag, but last year I had the best marks in the whole province, and I won a big scholarship—a really big one—just a few weeks ago. It will pay for me to study in France, at La Sorbonne. I go in the spring, start taking preparatory courses. I almost hate to go away, leave my Mom." She stopped suddenly and when she spoke again, I could barely hear her. "I really loved my father."

I never know what to do when a girl cries. Usually, I just get the heck out of the general area. This was Antonine, though. I felt like I needed to do something. I reached out for her as she walked slightly in front of me, but I just couldn't find the right way to do what needed to be done. I felt awfully awkward. So, I just let her keep talking, sobbing a little now as she spoke. I felt like such a useless jerk.

"He was an incredible man—strong and kind and smart. He made sure I knew all about Acadian history,

the legends around here; American history too, and
Canadian, and Mi'kmaw. He learned French, and
insisted that I be bilingual. Nearly tri-lingual actually.
That helped a lot getting the scholarship."

Now I felt like I wasn't just a jerk, but an idiot as well.
I used to be at the top of my classes too, or near them,
but I had let that slide, all because I'd allowed myself to
be buried in my own problems. And of course, I spoke
just one measly language.

We had reached the main road. Antonine stopped
and cast her gaze along one of the paths that led to the
other beach, the one we had been on earlier that looks
out toward the bay and the horizon.

"I saw the ghost ship one time before, when I was
a little girl, with Dad." She stopped and paused for a
while. "I've been coming here ever since, looking for it
on certain days in certain kinds of weather. It is amazing
that you and I saw it two days in a row. I did not think
that was possible. You just happened to come along and
so did the ship. I wonder if that means something...
other than that thing about lives being entwined."

She looked at me, her eyes still glazed with tears, her
face and black hair barely visible in the night. It was
strange though, I felt like I could see her clearly, not with
my eyes, but with my heart or my mind...or...something.

"I was just a little girl. Dad and Mom used to take me for walks on the beach here, since we did not have enough money to do many other things, travel, or even often go to the movies. We usually went to the less-crowded areas. For some reason, that day, about twelve or thirteen years ago, it was just Dad and me on our walk. I cannot remember why. Mom must have had a meeting or something. The weather was the way it is today, the way it was earlier, kind of readying itself for a storm, the sun about to set. I remember it like it was yesterday."

She paused again and looked toward the beach once more with a distant expression, as if she were still searching for something out on the water.

"We saw the ship. I remember he was carrying me and we were laughing and he just stopped suddenly and set me down gently onto my feet. 'What is it, Daddy?' I asked him. Then we heard distant screaming. It was a woman's voice, a young one, it seemed. It was way out on the water but we could hear her, I swear it. Maybe it was just the whistling of the wind, but if I were asked to say what it was in a court of law, I would say it was a girl. We just stood there staring for a moment. You could see it was a ship. So much like a ship! Much more than what you and I saw. We could see the burning timber of the hull, the sails, and something out on the bow."

That really freaked me out. I hadn't told her what I'd seen. I hadn't wanted to upset her even more than she already was, or sound like a lunatic.

I told myself, right there and then, that I definitely could not have seen a woman on the bow of that ghost ship.

"Dad took me by the hand and started to run, just like I did tonight." Antonine was almost in a trance now, her eyes focused on something not of this world. "He took me to the dock, just like we did, started a boat, like I did, and we roared out into the bay. That thing didn't look ghostly like it did tonight, Dylan, it looked real! We went after the fire like an arrow toward a target, the sound of the woman screaming growing louder and shooting across the waves toward us, the fire crackling behind her voice. But we couldn't get close. The heat was too much for us. She was burning alive!"

Antonine stopped for a moment and hung her head. "We had to pull back. Maybe Dad did that because I was with him and he didn't want to risk my life."

She lifted her head again. "We had neared a little island out in the bay. As we pulled away, we saw the ship starting to go down and what looked like a figure in the water, on fire, struggling to stay afloat."

A shiver ran down my spine. I could almost see it.

"Then everything went quiet," continued Antonine. "I remember that so well. There was near silence on the water, just the sound of the waves hitting our boat." She stopped for a moment and listened to the wind whistling around us on the beach. "Dad motored over to the place where the boat had been. I remember he reached down and pulled something out of the water. I don't know what it was, I didn't ask, I was too terrified, and he didn't say a word, he just took me into his arms and held me there all the way back to shore."

I actually felt a sense of relief, glad that they were safe.

"I remember," said Antonine, "that when we got back, there were people on the busier part of the beach who had been watching the fire on the water, and when we drove back into Bathurst, there were still onlookers standing on the bridge that goes into town, talking animatedly and staring out over the bay. It was the most spectacular sighting ever of the ghost ship of Chaleur Bay."

"Wow," was all I said.

Another lame comment from Dylan Maples.

"My father didn't say another word about that night for as long as he lived."

Uh-oh, I thought, *he's dead*.

"He never even mentioned it to Mom, at least not that I'm aware of. It was as if he hoped his little girl would think it was a dream. Maybe he thought he'd somehow experienced a hallucination himself."

"What about you?" I asked. "What did you believe?"

"I don't know. I still don't know. Maybe my child's mind made it much more than it was, but that is difficult for me to accept. I have had many nightmares about it over the years. I dream of raging fires on the bay, of legless pirates on the ship, and of a girl, screaming as she walks on water, fully engulfed in flames."

Man, I wished I could hug her, just reach out and do it, but I was pretty sure that no matter how I did it, it would be awkward. She looked so incredible in that dim, windy night, her black hair blowing around her face again.

I wanted to shake my head to wake myself up, but she was looking at me. We both turned at the sound of a car approaching, and then Antonine hurried to finish her story.

"My father never slept well after that either. I think it affected his health. He never felt he could say anything about what he had seen. He was a black man in a mostly white community and though most had treated him well, some did not. He often wondered if his race affected his ability to get a full-time job, though he never once complained around me. But he couldn't utter a word about what we'd seen on the bay. We had been so close to that apparition, seen the burning woman, and people on board! No one would believe a story about a phantom so detailed, so *real*, especially if it was told by a black man who wanted to be accepted in his community. I think he also feared that having such a vision was indeed insane. I should have talked to him about it."

She dropped her head and let out a sob.

The car stopped not far from us. Our family vehicle. Dad was behind the wheel. Mom jumped out and came marching toward us.

"Dad died exactly a month ago today," finished Antonine.

"Dylan!"

The "coming" thing was definitely not going to be of any use right now.

"The parental units," I explained.

"What?"

"My Mom and Dad."

"Goodbye," said Antonine. She turned and walked off the road and into the trees in the growing storm. It was as if she had vanished again.

9

THE TRUTH OUTS, SORT OF

It didn't go well with Mom, to say the least. Dad was trying to act like a go-between, be the reasonable one, but she shut him down fast.

"I guess you want to know," she said in a heated voice, each word emphasized by the heavy steps she was taking toward me, "what it would be like to be grounded when you are away from home, young man!" She was trying to keep her hair out of her face, but it was blowing around in the wind like a hurricane on her head.

"Laura, perhaps that's a little—"

"Oh, shut up, John!"

Wow, I'd never heard either of them say anything like that to each other. This did not bode well for me.

I turned toward the car, but Mom was just getting started. She stepped in front of me, blocking my escape.

"What in God's name have you been doing? You look like you were out sailing on the bay in the storm or something!"

"Right, Mom. Don't be ridiculous."

Oh, that wasn't a good thing to say, not good at all.

"Excuse me?"

"He said," began Dad, "not to be ridic—"

"I heard what he said!"

"I'm sorry, Mom, I just went for a long walk."

She examined my face. "Was someone with you, just now?"

"No." I had no idea why I lied.

"I thought there was," said Dad, "why would anyone want to be out here in this?"

It was starting to rain now, pelting down.

"A good question," said Mom, "for once."

Man, she was being totally irrational, but it was hard to blame her. The Bill and Bonnie Show was probably out somewhere looking for me. This had to be more than a little embarrassing for her. I also had the feeling that bringing me out to New Brunswick had been mostly her idea and now it seemed like it wasn't going well. One thing I knew about my Mom, and my Dad, was that they loved me. I know that doesn't sound like a cool thing to say, but it is true. It was tearing her apart that I hadn't been myself for a long while. I needed to be good to her.

"I'm sorry, Mom," I said again. "I think I'm working some things out. This trip has been good for me."

"Really?" said Dad.

Mom gave him a look and then turned back to me. It was raining harder now and we were getting soaked. A little smile crept over her lips. That was a relief.

"Really?" she asked quietly.

"Yeah." I am not a very good liar and I wasn't sure that she bought it, but it helped to take the edge off things for the time being.

WHEN WE GOT BACK to the house, Bill and Bonnie were there and looking relieved to see that I was alive, though I detected Bill wasn't too pleased with me. I was likely wrecking his hosting reputation...and cutting into his time to spread his theories and make himself look good.

I got changed and was on my best behavior throughout the meal they had all, again, waited to eat with me. I made sure I was polite and tried to look really interested in everything Bill said. It seemed to work. Even during a little rant about how self-concerned young people are ("with apologies to you, of course, Dylan," he said), I made sure I nodded. He knew a lot about being self-concerned.

THE NEXT DAY, ALL four of them watched me like hawks. All eight of them, to be exact, since the dogs seemed to spend most of their time camped in the hallway near my escape door, as if to say, "Going out sometime?"

When breakfast was over, the non-canine adults announced plans to make a trip to the beach "together," which meant I was going too. I wondered if they had planned that long before they told me. Maybe they talked about how I seemed to be fascinated by the beach and decided they could make me feel included by simply accompanying me, perhaps causing me to not want to get away from them too. That sounded like the sort of thing Bill would come up with—a calculated move disguised as kindness.

I, of course, was thinking about Antonine. I really hoped she would be there again, like she had said she would. Though I wondered if now that the ghost ship had made its appearance and she had told me her story, she would ever show up again. I also wondered, somewhere in the back of my head, if she was real at all.

Still, I had to find a way to get away on my own at least one more time, and see if she would be there. So, I decided to make a move. I made up my mind to do something really strange...I was going to tell the truth.

As everyone adjourned to their rooms to get ready for the beach, I knocked on Mom and Dad's door.

"Can I talk to you?" I asked. Low voice, sound a little upset, but not enough to raise alarm. That should work just fine.

"Sure, champ," said Dad.

I sat down on their bed and they sat on either side of me. It was like a pivotal scene in a heartwarming movie.

"I really do think that I am doing better," I said.

"That's great, Dylan," said Mom, holding my hand.

"I know I have to try to be more social, and accept what happened to Bomb, and make an effort to have some more friends in school, and I'm thinking that maybe I should even go back to playing hockey."

Mom smiled.

"But I have a confession."

Her smile came to a halt.

"I lied to you."

Her halted smile turned into a frown.

"There was someone with me last night."

I was getting to the key moment. I had to navigate

very carefully here. If I did it right, unveiled things in the correct way, this could work out very well. If not, I would be in a deeper pile of crap than I already was.

"What?" she said.

"When you found me on the beach."

"I thought so," said Dad. "Who was it?" he demanded.

"A girl."

"A girl?" asked Mom. It was hard to tell if she was relieved or upset.

"I met a girl, Mom, a really nice one. Her name is Antonine. She is from around here, part Acadian. I really like her."

Wow, this was a lot of confessing, but I hoped it would win me the twin-prizes of their sympathy and permission to spend more time with Antonine, even seek her out if she wasn't at Youghall today.

"I've seen her several times since we've been here. That's why I've been late getting back each time."

"That's great, Dylan!" said Dad. "Very exciting."

Mom gave him a bit of a look. "What do you mean by that?" she asked him.

"Uh, nothing," he said.

Good choice, Dad.

"She's a very nice person," I continued. "I think she is good for me...and I'd like to spend more time with her."

There was silence for a moment.

"Well," said Mom finally, "firstly, I appreciate that you told us the truth. It couldn't have been easy to admit to your deception."

Bingo.

"And secondly, We'd love to meet her." That meant Mom wanted to check her out. "And once we've said hello, I don't see why, all things going well, you can't see her again. Even if you have to miss an outing or two with us and Bonnie and Bill to do so."

Bingo again.

"Hey, man," said Dad, "an Acadian girlfriend. High five!"

He held up his hand, but by the look on Mom's face, I had a feeling I shouldn't return his offer.

"Or…" he continued, "yes…let's meet her and go from there."

"Well," I replied, "she said she would be at the beach this morning."

IT WAS A MUCH happier Maples family that walked down to the beach with the Bill and Bonnie Show later that morning.

The happiness didn't last, though. Antonine was nowhere to be seen.

10

PLEASE DON'T GO

I had to find her, even if she was a dream. I wasn't going to just let her slip out of my life, not now. And man, I had done a beautiful thing, great moves, in getting Mom and Dad on side when it came to her. I had set them up perfectly. They could tell how disappointed I was she wasn't at the beach and they actually seemed a little disappointed, too, so it was easy to convince them that I should make an effort to find her.

Bill and Bonnie were zero help.

"Antonine Marie Clay?" said Bill. "Jackson Clay? Never heard of him or her."

I had the feeling he didn't know many locals; none of the "average" people around here, even though he was such a big advocate for their "way of life" and this politician who was for "the little guy." Bill said Antonine's name as if she were fiction or a character I had made up. I wanted to kick him in the groin.

We spent the rest of the morning doing nothing, in my opinion, just walking along the beach and then coming back to Bill and Bonnie's deck and eating. I suppose it was all right just hanging out in this beautiful setting but I didn't want to be with the adults right then and I couldn't muster up the deception to fake it. Mom could tell. Bill and Bonnie, of course, didn't have a clue about what was wrong with me, though Bonnie was trying to be extra nice.

"I hope you're having a good time," she said as she handed me a lemonade.

I gave her a barely audible "yes."

About an hour or so after lunch, Mom surprised me.

"I think this calls for a single visit to your phone," she said quietly, as we moved down the hallway toward our rooms.

A few minutes later, she quietly knocked and handed me my phone when I opened the door.

"See if you can find Antonine's address. You know her last name and chances are she lives in Bathurst. Her parents probably have a landline."

"Parent," I said.

"I'm sorry?"

"Her dad is dead. It would just be her mom."

"Oh…that's too bad. Well, if you can find where she lives, I'll take you there."

I couldn't believe she said that. I searched 411 and found a single Clay, right in Bathurst as Mom suspected.

She let the others know that we were going out for a drive and we went into town and soon found Antonine's house, using Mom's phone for directions. Mom seemed really happy, though I didn't know whether it was helping me or finally getting a chance to use her cell for something.

Antonine's house wasn't very big—in fact, it was very small—and most of the other houses on her street weren't exactly mansions, to say the least. There were lots of trucks parked in driveways and people in work boots on the gravel sidewalks. But one thing I will say, her house looked like a home. It was neat and tidy, painted a happy yellow and the lawn was freshly cut and there were lots of bright flowers growing in the beds at the front of the house.

Mom pulled up and cut the engine.

"Away you go," she said.

I didn't move. My heart was pounding. For some reason, this was making me really nervous. I could say it was because I was arriving unannounced, that I was concerned that Antonine might be mad at me for almost stalking her all the way to her house, but I knew it was something else.

"Go on," said Mom as she reached over and patted my knee.

I got out without saying a word, approached the front door, walked up the three steps, and held my hand out to knock. I could hear two voices inside, two people talking in French. One of them was Antonine. I just listened for a while. She sounded incredible. I knocked.

There was silence for a moment and then a woman came to the door.

"Oui?" she said, looking surprised to greet a young stranger. I could see Antonine in her green eyes and strong build, but her hair was blonde.

"Uh, Dylan Maples." I kind of wheezed it out.

"Pardon?" She pronounced it the French way.

"I'm...I'm Dylan Maples. Is Antonine here?"

"Antonine? May I ask what you want?"

Antonine appeared in the hallway behind her, looking shocked. She was dressed up a bit, her hair done up, as if she had just returned from school.

"Dylan?" she said. She didn't sound happy.

"Can I come in?"

"No," said Antonine, "I'll come out."

Her mother smiled at her as she walked past, a look of curiosity in her eyes.

When we got outside, Antonine noticed the car parked out front.

"My mom," I explained.

She motioned for me to follow her around to the back of the house. The lawn there was really small too, but there was a good-sized shed and lots of kids' playground equipment scattered about, and all of them looked homemade—wooden slides, ladders, and a cool little playhouse.

"Wow," I said. "My dad made them." She looked down at the ground. "He used to work in that shed. It was his special place. He would go in there some mornings and only come out to eat, it seemed. It's kind of closed up now. We don't go in there."

"I—"

"Dylan, why did you come here? How did you find me?"

"Uh, I used my phone."

"Oh, yeah, of course. I don't have a cellphone."

"You what?"

"I bet you use yours all the time."

"Uh, yeah, a bit."

"What do you want?"

This wasn't going very well.

"Uh, I just want to know...how you're doing. How are you?"

Lame.

"I'm fine. Had a bit of a headache for a while from bonking my head, but I am okay. Dylan, what do you want, really?"

"I want to...just hang out. I want...to know more about the ghost ship."

"That's the problem with you being here."

"What do you mean?"

"My mom doesn't know anything about Dad and I and the ghost ship. I told you, he didn't ever tell her. I was scared you were going to blurt something out there at the door, and I have been thinking about it anyway, and I've decided it isn't good for me to dwell on what happened back then. It only makes me unhappy. I have been kind of obsessed with it. Besides, I really don't remember it that well. How could I, since I was only four years old? Dad couldn't have seen what he claimed he saw. He must have put all that in my head. It wasn't a proud moment for him, that hallucination. It may have been something messing with his mind because he was upset about other things. I want to think of my father as a good man...a sane man."

She looked really sad.

"That doesn't mean we can't be friends," I said.

"Dylan, that illusion on the water only appears to people maybe every few years, if that. I saw it with you on two consecutive days! The moment you appeared, it did. You remind me of the burning ghost ship of Chaleur Bay. You always will. You will remind me of a very strange moment—and not a good moment—in my father's life."

Girls have really interesting ways of telling you to piss off.

"Yeah," I said.

Good start, Dylan. Maybe add a word or two?

"Yeah...but...." I can be an awfully eloquent guy sometimes.

"It's the truth," she said.

"I don't care," I sputtered. "I don't want to lose you as a friend."

Wow! Where did that come from? Not from Dylan Maples, but from some sort of unknown, invisible force inside me that had at least some courage, that knew I had to have this friend.

Her eyes went a little moist. Man, had I just said a really good thing to a girl?

"You are a special guy, Dylan," she said.

Wow and wow again. I was putting the moves on her without even knowing it, I think. I had not thought of myself as being in any way a "special guy" for a long time. Then, I almost blew it.

"So are you," I said.

She laughed out loud. "A special guy? I'm a special guy? Thanks, Dylan."

But she wasn't mad. She was smiling at me, a priceless sort of smile that was both in her lips and her eyes, which were looking at me in a kind of intense way.

"Could...could I see you again?" I asked.

That sounded way too grown-up for me, for Dylan Maples. I had seen men ask women that in movies. What does it really mean? No one needs to ask permission to see others, to literally observe them. I was seeing her right now!

"Uh," she said, "I'll think about it."

"Okay," I said.

She smiled again.

THE NEXT DAY WAS probably the most boring in the history of Dylan Maples. No Antonine. No phone. Just the parental units and the Bill and Bonnie Show. We only had a few days left in New Brunswick. I kept wondering how to work this. Should I just charge over to her house—I had memorized how to get there and figured I could walk it in about a couple of hours, maybe less—or should I wait for her to make her move? And if she did make a move, how would she be able to do it? Did she have Bill and Bonnie's phone number? Did she know where they lived? How would she contact me?

Then I realized she was just being nice to me. How in the world could I have ever believed that someone like Antonine would have the least bit of interest in me? Dylan Maples! She had just been putting me off. She didn't know how to contact me. She didn't care.

Then I wondered if I should be going to Youghall Beach, where we had met. I headed downstairs to ask permission to go there on my own—a wise move under the circumstances—and couldn't find anyone. I went out the front door and discovered Mom and Bonnie walking around outside, inspecting the house and gardens. I heard Bonnie saying something about how "wonderfully New Brunswick" it all was. Dad and Bill were apparently off on a walk, "looking at properties," as Bonnie put it. The dogs were following the ladies about with spit-soaked tennis balls in their mouths, colour-coded for each pet, slobbering on the humans' pant legs, shoving the balls into their mistress's and guest's personal areas.

"They are such darlings," laughed Bonnie.

Mom looked like she wanted to brain them.

I sidled up to her. "Can I, uh," I said quietly, hoping Bonnie couldn't hear exactly what I was saying. She seemed to lean toward us, though. "Can I go to the beach?"

I almost felt like I should wink at Mom. But she got it right away.

"Sure," she said. Then she moved a little closer. "Have fun, Romeo," she whispered into my ear. Her jokes are sometimes a little inappropriate.

I went to the beach feeling nervous, but there was no need. I couldn't find Antonine—and believe me, I looked everywhere. Then it struck me that—duh!—she was in school. I waited for hours, long past the end of the school day, but she didn't show.

I actually went the next morning, too, even though it was a Friday, somehow wildly hoping she would just take time away from school to see me. I got permission from Dad, who was reading a newspaper when I inquired—some old people still do that. He waved me on my way with one of his smiles, likely not hearing a single detail of what I asked for; I could have been telling him that I was heading out to swim with sharks. Not that he doesn't care. I know he does. He had been quite interested in my affection for Antonine. It's just his weird concentration thing.

"Make a good speech at my funeral!" I called back to him at the door. He smiled again and waved me off.

Antonine wasn't at Youghall that morning either. It made sense, but when three o'clock came she still wasn't there, and I had heard Bill complaining that school ended early on Fridays in their region. I started to get upset, my heart throbbing as I walked back to the house. We were running out of time.

I went to my room and closed the door. Mom didn't dare bother me about it. She could tell what the problem was and knew it wasn't fair to pester me right now.

"Hey, man," said Bomber, "swipe your phone from your parents' room and text the guys to tell them what's going on. It's good to talk about these things. Friends, man, can't be beat."

"Not now, Bomb," I whispered.

I closed my eyes, tried to pretend he wasn't sitting on the end of my bed. I heard Mom and Dad talking to Bill and Bonnie down in the living room, planning another day trip, this time longer, up north Campbellton way.

Then the doorbell rang.

A minute later Mom was at my door, a big smile on her face.

"There's someone here to see you."

11

A GIFT

Antonine was standing a few feet back from the front door, taking in Bill and Bonnie's fancy house with an uncertain look, as if wondering whether she should even be here.

"Hi," she said.

Wow, I thought, *she actually seems a bit nervous.*

Was it really possible that this fascinating girl was nervous about seeing Dylan Maples? Maybe seeing him, but not me. The units were both gazing at her with huge smiles, which I thought was a bit much.

"Come on in," I said.

"I'd rather not. Could we go to the beach?"

I didn't have any problem convincing Mom and Dad

to allow us to go. In fact, they even let me off of the big trip to Campbellton. The four of them were planning to have lobster somewhere and visit some things that had to do with the Battle of Restigouche—which actually sounded pretty cool—and I was going to miss that, but I could tell Mom and Dad thought it was important for me to have time with Antonine.

Bill and Bonnie didn't look too pleased about me missing the trip. They came out to the door and had a proper introduction to Antonine, but they seemed kind of snobby about it, or at least Bill did. On the surface they were all warm and friendly but Bill took a look at my friend in her plain T-shirt and jeans and didn't even bother to shake her hand or say anything more than "hello" and "how nice to meet you" and that sort of crap. They didn't ask her one word about where she lived or what school she went to or anything like that, though Bonnie did add that she hoped to see her again.

TEN MINUTES LATER, ANTONINE and I were on the beach, well rid of the adults, at least the Bill and Bonnie part, though Dad had nearly embarrassed the pants off me by wishing me a "great time, champ," right in front of Antonine.

"What are you the champ of?" she asked with a grin as we hit the sand.

"Anyone's guess."

We didn't talk very much at first, just walked along the beach toward Youghall, which was kind of our area, I suppose. It was funny, usually when I'm with someone and there isn't a lot of talking, it feels really uncomfortable, but it didn't with her. We just walked, fairly close to each other, saying nothing, for the most part just looking out at the water.

When we got to Youghall, we sat down on a log and then really started to talk.

"I think we should investigate the ghost ship," I said. I figured that was a daring thing to say, given how much she didn't even want the topic brought up.

She just stared at me for moment. I was sure I'd blown it. Finally, she sighed. "You are probably right. I should face this whole thing. Maybe if I learn more about it and think about why my Dad might have thought he interacted with an illusion, I can live with it a little better."

"Do you want to talk more about your dad? About what happened at the end?" That was another tough subject, but I had the feeling that she hadn't discussed it at all, with anyone, and needed to express her feelings about it. It was as if I were suddenly that Dr. Phil guy on TV, exploring a personal issue for someone. I was definitely not Dylan Maples.

At first she didn't respond to that either, but then she started to speak and everything came out in a waterfall of words.

"Like I said, it was only about a month ago. He had not been feeling well for a while. He was never particularly good with stress and we were having a hard time financially, getting calls from the banks. We are fine now that he's gone. Life insurance."

She could barely get that out, but she steeled herself and kept talking. She was tough. I thought of how little she had said about her headache after knocking herself woozy in the boat.

"He never really fit in here. Even though we are such a mixture of people and think we are so welcoming, I can actually name people who treated him differently from others because he was black. He could feel it. He just kept working, though, day after day at his part-time teaching job. He was pretty embarrassed by that, since he had such a good position in Alabama. He never said so, he was quite an old-fashioned man about it all, but I could tell."

She paused again for a while.

"He was such an amazing dad. I believe he is still here, with me and Mom."

"I have a friend like that."

"What do you mean?"

"Someone who died."

"Tell me about him."

"He was just a guy; a goof like me. His name was Bomb Connors."

"Bomb? That's cool."

I could have kissed her for that. Although, I could have kissed her for just being alive and sitting there, too.

"He was killed in a head-on collision on the big highway that runs through Toronto. What are the chances of that?"

"Not good."

"It kind of…broke my heart." Holy crap, I couldn't believe I said that, nor could I believe that tears were welling in my eyes. This was an emergency! I looked out over the water and tried to remember some Leafs stats.

"That's understandable," she said…and took my hand.

Holy, holy, holy, holy.

You cannot imagine what that felt like. I knew she was strong and likely played lots of sports and yet her hand felt like it was made of cream or something. I just about fell off the log. She squeezed my hand and then let go. That was probably a good thing since I was literally speechless when she was touching me. If she had asked me anything then I would probably have sounded like Chewbacca when I answered.

"Your friend is still with you, Dylan," Antonine said. "The most important things in life are the invisible things, the things that touch your heart. Dad used to say that all the time. We all get caught up in visible things…you know, clothes, money, businesses, politics, that sort of thing, the way we look, what race we are, what culture we're from. Dad said those things weren't important. He used to insist that you needed to hold on to what mattered to you deep inside and that was all that was important in the end. He was a very spiritual man. I believe all those things he said. He is with me. He walks beside me every day. To be honest…I see him sometimes—as alive as he was in life—a sort of ghost. I've never told Mom that."

"I…I see Bomber sometimes, too." I didn't tell her how vivid it was and that he talked to me when I was really down, or about Grandpa's ghost, or the one I'd seen in Newfoundland, because I didn't want her to think I was really nuts.

She smiled. Then she sighed. "I don't get along too well with other kids in my school, at least I haven't recently. I have always felt different. I have a few friends, but no one close, so keeping my dad, my best friend, in my heart, is pretty important."

Wow, I thought, *how could this person not have many friends?*

"No boyfriend?" I asked. Man, my mouth had been out of control lately. I seemed to be saying any crap that came into my head. Do any guys ever come up to girls and just ask them if they have a boyfriend?

"No," she said, and she blushed a little.

"That's hard to believe," I said. I had no idea who was talking. It certainly wasn't Dylan Maples or me. It was some guy from the movies or something, who I was imitating. Somehow, I just felt compelled to say these things to her.

"Thanks," she said, very quietly. "But I don't have a lot of time for boys. Schoolwork is what matters to me. Both Mom and Dad drilled that into me."

"Oh, yeah," I said, "top marks in the school, right?"

"That's right." She looked proud, not an ounce of embarrassment. I thought that was very cool too. I could not help again reflecting on how I had let my marks slip lately. I made a little vow to do better.

We didn't say anything more for a while. We were both looking out over the water toward the horizon where we had encountered that illusion, that ball of fire. I wondered why I had seen it. Was I that upset about things? Had I desperately wanted to see what Antonine had seen?

"I've been struggling for a while now," I whispered. I had stopped thinking that it wasn't me talking. It was Dylan Maples and me, one and the same. "It's almost gotten to be like social anxiety or something. I spend a lot of time in my room. And I'm not the nicest person these days, pretty cynical, I guess. We came out here so I could get away from things."

"And you met me," she smiled.

"Yes."

"And you saw the burning ghost ship of Chaleur Bay...twice. You and I saw it together." She didn't have to say anything else. I remembered the legend about intertwined fates.

"Antonine...I know I said we should check out the ghost ship more and I know we saw something, both nights, something weird, but I really find it hard to believe that it was anything other than an illusion of some sort, or just a fire on the water."

I knew I wasn't being honest with her. When she'd been lying dazed on the boat the other night, I knew I'd seen an actual ship on fire and a burning woman too. I had heard her screaming. I just didn't want to admit it. I think I was desperate not to.

"I told you what Dad and I saw when we were close to it. You can laugh at me if you want," she said.

"No," I replied instantly, "I...I believe you. I...have a confession." I took a deep breath. "I saw something in detail as well, the night we chased after it...after you hit your head...it looked like a woman on fire at the front of a ship too." I sighed. "I just haven't been able to tell you."

Her eyes had been defiant. Now they softened.

"Thank you for telling me now."

"I think we need to try to figure this out, Antonine, somehow."

"Would you do that with me?"

I felt like saying I would do anything with her, but I just nodded. Her eyes grew a little misty again. She reached a hand toward her throat and pulled out the pendant on the necklace she was wearing. I had noticed the small glittering silver chain before, which hung down under her T-shirt. I saw now that the pendant was a small silver cross. She reached behind her neck and pretended to take the whole necklace off.

"My father gave this to me," she said so quietly that I could barely hear her. "I could never part with it. But somehow, I want you to have it too."

She reached over, her face up very close to mine, smelling like lavender or something, and pretended to put the invisible necklace around my neck and fasten it.

It was funny. I could feel it hanging there.

"Please," she said, "don't ever take it off."

I swallowed. Even Alice had never offered me anything like this.

12

INVESTIGATION

Antonine suggested we go to the Bathurst Public Library first. Her mom worked there and was familiar with all the resources. She knew there was a whole collection about the burning ghost ship, though she had never been able to bring herself to go through it. The only problem was that the library was in downtown Bathurst, a long way from Youghall Beach. I was wondering if Mom would drive us. But if we did that, I'd have to explain what we were doing.

"Let's walk," said Antonine, "the library is open late today."

"Walk?" I said. "How far is it?"

She was already on her feet.

"About an hour and a half."

"An hour and a half!" I realized that earlier I had actually considered walking all the way to her house, which was even farther, but that was when I was missing her and the trek was just a possibility.

"Yes, city boy. I walk out here lots of times."

"Even when you could take the bus or ride your bike?"

"Or take the subway?"

We started walking.

IT WAS SURPRISING HOW little time it seemed to take. Maybe it had something to do with the company. We just talked up a storm as we strolled along, as if we had known each other since we were kids. She quizzed me about living in Toronto and had all sorts of weird ideas about it as if it were a gigantic, scary place.

"Aren't there lots of murders there, like all the time?"

"Uh…it's a very big city so sometimes bad things happen and they get a lot of attention, but I've never heard of a single murder anywhere near where I live, ever, in history. I don't think I've even heard of a fist fight nearby."

"Really? Ever?" She paused. "There was actually a sort of bad fight between some of *our* neighbours last week. It got kind of physical. I couldn't sleep."

"Well, I've read that, statistically, Toronto is one of the safest places in all of Canada. I bet it is even safer than Bathurst, per pop."

I didn't know if that was true, but I wouldn't be surprised.

"People here always say that Toronto isn't very friendly."

That was something I had heard lots of others say during the trips we'd taken around Canada.

"That's not even remotely true. Have any of those people ever lived in Toronto? If they haven't, then what are they basing their opinions on? People in my city are as nice as any place I have ever been."

As I defended my hometown, I realized how lucky I was to live in such a big, interesting place where I felt safe. It also made me think about how people judge places and other people by appearances and stories they hear.

"That's a good point," said Antonine. "I should know better than to listen to that sort of thing. I'd like to visit you sometime."

Well, my friend, I would love it if you did, I thought, but I didn't let that one out of my mouth.

She told me more about her life, too. At first, it sounded kind of bleak, mostly because she just talked about the last few months, but once we got into her whole life in Bathurst, you could tell she was proud of where she lived, too.

"This whole area is just so beautiful, and mostly really friendly. The countryside and the water, the bay, just get inside you. It's neat that it's a tourist destination for lots of Canadians, a place where people want to come. I'm really going to miss it when I go to France."

That stopped our conversation for a few minutes, but it didn't take us long to get going again. Our whole chat cheered up both of us. It occurred to me that lately I had been thinking of my entire life as if it was just the last year.

We talked about things on social media, too, but that didn't go very far because she hardly knew anything about it. I had forgotten that she didn't have a phone. You just kind of assume all other kids have them.

"I like movies, though," she offered.

"So do I."

"My favourites are old ones like *Gone With the Wind* and *Notting Hill*; anything ancient that's good. Mom and I like to watch them together at home."

Didn't know those ones.

"How about *Star Wars*?"

I'm not sure why I said that because I'm not particularly caught up in that whole franchise. I suppose

I was just clutching at straws to find something we both might have seen.

"I'm not a big fan," she said after a bit of a pause, "I'm not really into science fiction stuff. I have seen some of them though and my favourite part is when they talk about the Force. I love the Force. To me, it is the most interesting thing about those films."

"I think that, too," I said, and it was true. We smiled at each other.

We passed by the gorgeous golf course that was at the edge of the bay and then turned onto a busy street with big-box stores and fast-food restaurants, and walked along there until we came to the bridge that was stretched over the water and into the main part of old Bathurst. To our left, we could see Youghall Beach in the distance and Chaleur Bay beyond it.

It didn't take us long to get from there to the library, which was downtown in a big modern brick building that was apparently built the year they had the Canada Winter Games here. It was relatively new and therefore stuck out on the street.

It was a nice, bright space inside and Antonine knew everyone, saying hello in both French and English—it was so cool hearing her speak another language so easily—until we reached her mother's desk where the two of them really lit up to see each other and hugged.

"I guess I didn't introduce you properly to my mom before," said Antonine, turning to me. "Well, this is her, Madame Clay, children's librarian."

"Eve," said her mother, reaching out to me and taking my hand in both of hers. "Welcome to Bathurst, Acadia, and New Brunswick." She had an amazing French accent that made her words sound like parts of a song. "What are you two up to?"

"Doing some research," said Antonine.

"Really? About what?"

"The ghost ship."

For a second I wondered why she revealed what we were doing, but then remembered that her father had never told her mother about that night long ago.

"Oh, fascinating!" said Eve. "That's a great subject for a visitor! Makes us seem a little less boring here in Baie-des-chaleurs. You know, I never saw the ship. Lived here my whole life and never saw it once. Maybe that makes me unique."

"You are unique, Mom."

"That could mean a lot of things, my little one."

They laughed.

"Dylan gave up a trip to Campbellton and a lobster supper to hang out with me."

"Well," said Eve, "we can't have that. Lobster dinner at our house when you guys are done! I'll make a call and get some fresh."

THE LIBRARY HAD A mile of information about the burning ghost ship of Chaleur Bay in the local history section.

We made our way into that area and found what we were looking for on shelves that dominated part of the room, all sorts of things on the walls too, almost like advertisements. There were drawings and paintings of it on fire, laminated copies of newspaper articles that reported sightings, and even a photograph of a beer bottle from the region with the ghost ship sailing across the label.

We thought we would start out by investigating the different theories about the origins of the legend, the historical origins. What exactly was this ship and why was it in the bay?

"You know that stuff I told you on the beach?" said Antonine. "That's just what I've heard. We all know something about the phantom around here. The details about it, though, that's just scared me too much."

Now, however, she (and I) were ready to get into it. We went through books, newspaper articles, essays, and even doctoral theses and things from scientific journals. Some of it was hard to understand so we didn't exactly read every word, but by the time we were done, about an hour or so later, we had a pretty good picture of what we were dealing with.

There were a million theories about the ship. I stopped counting when I got past twenty. Probably the most popular one, which was even in a City of Bathurst tourism package with a burning ship logo on it, told the story that Antonine had given me in a sentence or two back on the beach. The details were fascinating: the bad guy was a Portuguese dude named Gaspar Corte-Real, a shady trader who tried to rip off the Mi'kmaq with trinkets and things in exchange for furs. He came here about 1501, sailing his three-masted ship into Chaleur Bay, grabbing some Mi'kmaw folks, and stealing them back to Europe to sell them into slavery. When he returned to New Brunswick a little later—which to me took a boatload of stones—the Mi'kmaq were ready for him. They boarded his ship, killed all his men, tied Gaspar to a rock, and waited until the tide came in and drowned him. They may have even had their lunch while they watched.

Now, I am not saying that was a nice thing, but man, he deserved it. Apparently, the story goes—and it was told in about fifty different ways in these library papers—Gaspar's brother, Miguel, came looking for him two years later and found his ship still anchored in the bay. But the Mi'kmaq were ready for him, too, and burned his vessel, along with him and everyone in it. Now, of course, it haunts the bay, on fire, sailors climbing the rigging and running along the decks to escape the flames.

Another great story in the collection had to do with a pirate named Captain Craig—you think he could have come up with a better handle than that, maybe like Captain Ugly-Beard or something—who captured two Mi'kmaw women in Chaleur Bay and intended to have his way with them, but an Acadian man helped them escape. Craig's craft was then shipwrecked, he and all his men died, and that very night it was seen shooting across the water, on fire. Wow, that was pretty cool.

There was also a story about the ship having taken part in the Battle of Restigouche in 1760, the very battle I was supposed to look into with Mom and Dad and the Bill and Bonnie Show in Campbellton. That conflict happened up the coast from Bathurst. In it, the British defeated the French, Acadians, and Mi'kmaq in one of the last battles to decide whether North America would become English or French.

There was a legend about a bride who was kidnapped and attacked by marauding sailors, whose souls now haunt the waters here in a floating inferno; and another about a couple of women being killed by buccaneers, who put a spell on their murderers, saying "may you burn on the bay forever," or something like that.

It was all wild stuff. There were patterns to it, too. Most of the stories dealt with ships from about 1500 to the late 1700s and many had to do with nefarious things done to Indigenous people, and often Indigenous women.

I kept thinking about what I had seen out there on the bay…a woman on fire at the bow of an ancient ship. I told myself it had to be my imagination.

Another thing that was common in the stories was location. Though these apparitions have been seen all the way up and down Chaleur Bay and the area from Caraquet in the south up to Campbellton in the north, most were observed pretty close to Bathurst and a number appeared off Youghall Beach. Some of them were on Heron Island, a bit more than half an hour up the coast, a short distance into the bay. Old settlers there used to say they had seen legless sailors with terrible burns near their houses. That was a pretty sick image, too.

It occurred to me that when Antonine and I had seen the ship, both times it had been to the north in the bay and moving up the shoreline in the direction of Heron Island.

The sheer amount of sightings was amazing and didn't fit into the normal profile of ghost appearances. As Antonine had said, phantoms usually appear to one person at a time, not to groups, but a high percentage of these sightings seemed to be viewed by more than one person, sometimes really large gatherings. One time it appeared in the middle of summer when Youghall Beach was crowded and everyone just stood there watching it! A mayor of Bathurst saw it twice and even took a picture. It was from far away though and didn't tell you much, just a light on the horizon.

"Imagine," I said to Antonine, "if someone could take a really good photograph of it. That would be spectacular and I bet it would make the person who snapped it a celebrity and probably rich." There was certainly nothing like that in the collection.

We moved on to the last part of our investigation, the scientific explanations. I was anxious to get to them, so everything could be explained and Antonine could stop worrying about this illusion and we could get onto just being friends...or more.

There were tons of explanations and many by experts with all sorts of fancy titles: doctors of various sciences, professors, and reputable journalists. Some dude from Harvard Medical School even chimed in. They wrote articles and papers about how the visual of a burning ship was caused by gases escaping from undersea fissures, or from rotting vegetation or marine life. Some speculated it was St. Elmo's fire—the "natural phenomenon" Antonine had mentioned—and others were sure it had to do with atmospheric conditions.

That last idea was interesting, since it branched off into weird things called "atmospheric ghost lights." There was apparently something called "will-o'-the-wisp," which was fire that appears out of nowhere over water or marshes, and may have to do with some sort of natural electrical phenomenon meeting up with natural gases...though some folk tales actually said it might come from spirits of the dead!

It was incredibly intriguing, but there was an undercurrent in it all that I found disturbing. No one was *sure* about this thing. Not that it existed; they all admitted to that. No one, however—Harvard Medical pooh-bah or ordinary citizen—was willing to say that there was an even remotely acceptable answer to what it really was. Not a single expert *knew*. Every one

of them said at the end of their articles that it was...
unexplainable. This thing that people were seeing,
constantly and in groups, was moving around out there
on the bay as some sort of unfathomable reality.

Wow.

When I left that room I was a little shaken. So was
Antonine and that upset me just as much, maybe more.
Though I could live with seeing my grandfather and
Bomber after they died—could explain their appearances
as a symptom of my anxiety—I didn't want to believe
that there was a ghost of this sort, this magnitude, in
our midst. A ghost that crowds had seen. A ghost both
Antonine and I had observed up close and personal. But
there seemed to be no reason to believe we hadn't.

I wondered what Antonine was thinking now. Had
her father, a relatively healthy and fairly young man,
been haunted to death by the sight of this thing and a
poor woman on fire on the bay near his chosen home?
We hadn't proven that Jackson Clay was of stable mind
and that must have been hurting her deep inside.

Then Florence Green showed up.

We were walking back toward Eve's desk, not saying
anything, and I was trying to look at the positive side
of things—I was about to have my first New Brunswick
lobster dinner with two amazing people.

"Hello, you two," said Eve.

There was another woman at her desk, a bit older, grey hair, dressed the way most folks around here dressed—in ordinary clothes, blue pants and a plain sweater, not putting on airs—and she had been deep in conversation with Antonine's mom.

"This is Florence Green," explained Eve. "I gave her a call and asked her to come over. She works as a volunteer at the Bathurst Heritage Museum on Douglas Avenue. She has a story for you."

"Hello there," said Florence.

Just two words and if I had come from the moon I would have known she was the genuine article. There was just something about her. It made me smile. She was friendly, welcoming, and absolutely herself. If she had told you that she had just returned from a trip to Planet Vulcan where she'd had tea with Harry Potter and Han Solo you would have believed her.

"Welcome to Bathurst!" she cried. She stood there and smiled at me, like the best aunt or grandma you could have. "I do indeed have a story for you. Well, not a story, actually, a true-to-life thing."

AND THIS IS WHAT Florence the down-to-earth grandma told us.

"I saw your ghost ship, I did, when I was a youngster. Not a child or anything like that, I was a young lady, in my twenty-second year. In those days, I used to live in the western part of Bathurst. I'd taken a college degree in Saint John and come back here, looking for a man likely—and I landed one eventually—but set up as a schoolteacher at first. That's what I was in one of my earlier incarnations. Anyway, I used to walk into town here to the old theatre to see the pictures. I was a James Dean fan, gosh he was beautiful. I'd slip in here, sometimes with a fella or even with a girlfriend or two, and see a movie and then walk back out of town."

"Those were the days," said Eve with a smile.

"They were indeed, my dear, but this particular night, it was in the summer, there was a storm brewing, you could tell by the feel of the air, and I was hurrying along the street back toward home, and started heading out across the bridge from the main part of town out to the west. You may know that Chaleur Bay is then on your right, and you can see clear across it from there almost out into the Gulf of St. Lawrence. I was motoring along on the bridge when suddenly it seemed to me that some extra streetlights had come on. I looked up and then out over the water and I saw it. The burning ghost ship of Chaleur Bay!"

I tried not to look at Antonine, but when I glanced over, she was glancing back at me.

"I find it hard to believe that it was ever as vivid as it was that night," continued Florence. "It was maybe a mile out but I could see it as clear as day. I stood there as if I was in some sort of trance and then realized that a car had stopped beside me, right on the bridge, and a man had gotten out. It was a taxi driver, Jean-Guy Knowles. 'That's it, ain't it, Flo?' he said to me, his voice sounding kind of weak for a big man like him. 'It sure is,' I think I said back. I don't remember much more about our conversation because I was just staring at the phantom ship. I couldn't believe what I was seeing, and by that I don't mean that I was all aghast at simply observing it. It was more than that. Oh my, much more! I could see that it had three masts, I could see the rigging, I could see the men climbing up on it as if trying to get away, others writhing on the deck, and out front on the bow, a woman...my gosh, yes, a woman, on fire! I could tell you everything you want to know about that ship: its colour, its size, even the sound of the timber crackling and the woman screaming."

She stopped suddenly. I realized when she looked at me that my mouth was wide open. I didn't dare turn to Antonine now.

"That's my story," said Florence Green with a shrug.

"A story, yes," I said quickly. "What…what do you believe causes it?"

"Causes it?"

"What is it? St. Elmo's fire? Atmospheric lights?"

"None of those."

"Then, what?" asked Antonine.

"It's real," Florence said.

"What?" said Eve.

"I have been a teacher and now I'm a pretty good amateur historian. I am a wife, a mother, and a grandmother. I do not believe in ghosts or anything airy-fairy in life. But I saw a burning ship that night, as sure as I'm standing here, and so did all the other folks who stopped their cars on the bridge and looked out at it."

"But surely you can't believe it was a ghost," I said. "You'd have to be able to explain it, wouldn't you?"

"I said I don't believe in ghosts and I stand by that. But sometimes I wonder," said Florence, "if there is something…in between."

Something in between.

13

A MEMORY

Dinner at the Clays' house was unbelievable, though I made a fairly serious mistake at the beginning. We ate in their little kitchen that had a big window that looked out over the backyard. Eve had cooked up a storm: amazing homemade bread cut really thick, potatoes fried in butter, corn on the cob, these weird little green vegetables she'd unfrozen especially for me to try called fiddleheads (apparently a New Brunswick thing) soaked in butter and salt too, and of course, the lobster. I wasn't too crazy about the fact that Eve got out a big pot and essentially boiled them alive, but that's what they do with lobster. And man, it was good. She and Antonine taught me how to eat it, how to crack open the bright-red shells to get the good meat and soak it in—you guessed it—butter, which Eve had melted and left in a little dipping bowl.

Before all of that, though, we had to set the table, of course. That was when I made my big mistake. I volunteered to help and Antonine got the plates and cutlery out and handed me some. She set her two plates on either side of the table and I, naturally, set one between them, at the head. Antonine stopped suddenly, as if she were frozen, and stared at what I had done. Eve just happened to be placing some food on the table at the same time.

"That's for my—" began Antonine.

"No," said Eve quickly, "no, that's fine. Go ahead, Dylan, you can sit at the head of the table. It's nice to have a man around the house again."

I felt like an idiot and wanted to clear the plate off the table with the back of my hand and smash it on the floor, but Eve was so nice about it that I didn't say a word.

A few minutes later, I lowered my butt into the chair as if Mr. Clay's revered place was going to disintegrate beneath me. Everything seemed fragile for a moment, but it didn't take long for us to get really chatting. They were just so incredibly nice and they weren't putting it on, they were simply that way. I felt like I'd always been a member of their family. It was so cool—me, this kid from Toronto, Eve, this Acadian lady from the Maritimes, Antonine, and the presence of her dad, all of us just talking as if we'd known each other all our lives.

I am a bit of a sap about this kind of thing—people of all different sorts getting along like a team. It was as if I was crying inside or something. Man, this really was something to *keep* inside. The whole scene was perfect, though. The way life should be.

At one point, we started talking about the upcoming by-election.

"I am not certain how I will vote," said Eve, "though I know for sure that it won't be for Jim Fiat. I knew him when he was a kid and he was a real little devil. His dad was the richest man around here and Jimmy inherited most of it, and now all he can talk about is being an 'average guy' against the powerful 'elite.' It is as if the people up in Ottawa are all evil. I'm guessing there are some nice folks there with honest intentions. It seems to me that he is just using whatever idea he can get his hands on to win the election. He is against more immigration, too, talks about it constantly, and I married an immigrant! I'm not crazy about the other parties, though. There just seems to be so much bickering. I wish we could all just respect each other, see each other as people and seek solutions. It is what is inside you that counts, not the outside. I may just sit this one out."

I could see where Antonine got her values. It was hard not to agree with Eve, though to be honest I didn't know much about politics, nor did I care. Bill got me riled up about it, but that was as much about his attitude as the issues themselves. I didn't like the next topic that came up either, though. It was about Antonine going away.

"So, I guess my little one has told you about how incredibly smart she is, and that she's going to France next year, abandoning me."

"Mom, not one word of what you just said is remotely true."

"When do you go?" I asked.

Antonine paused. "In the spring. I told you that."

Mom says I don't listen very well and sometimes she ties it to me being male. I argue with her about that, but she may be right.

"Oh, yeah," I said. When she had first talked to me about going away, I guess I hadn't found her quite as interesting as I did now. Is that a good way to put it? Anyway, I hadn't paid the sort of attention to detail I was paying now. She was going away in six months? Right out of the country?

"But you won't be finished high school, will you?"

"That's the way it works. They want you to start early there. You do a year of what is essentially high school and then start in at their university. I'm really excited about it."

I wasn't.

WE TALKED FOR SUCH a long time that the sun went down and we were still sitting at the table. I had eaten a boatload of food too, just piling it in, both of my hosts smiling at what I was able to hoover into me. It wasn't entirely my fault; the food was incredibly good. Eve didn't stop at a smoking first course either, she brought on a dessert that just seemed to glow when she set it down on the table. It was some sort of butter-tart pie, full of maple syrup and pecans and a crust that appeared to have a pound of butter in it. I think I had four pieces. I apologized for each of the last three. It was partly Eve's fault…she kept asking me if I wanted more.

Finally, unfortunately, it was time to go. The three of us piled into Eve's little car and they took me back to Bill and Bonnie's place. The lights were all on in their house and Mom came to the front door when we knocked, looking anxious. I guess I had been away for quite a long time again. Eve and Antonine didn't want to come in with me—I had the sense that all that money made them a little nervous—so they just waved from the car.

Though it had been a great evening, I went to bed that night on edge. Two things were bothering me: firstly, I only had two days left here and Antonine wasn't even going to be in the country shortly after that; and secondly, we had left the whole ghost ship thing hanging. We had seen something bizarre out there on the water, been close to it, and had found exactly zero confirmation that it was any sort of natural phenomenon. It had freaked out Antonine's father enough that it maybe contributed to his death. It had made him seem like he was crazy not just back then, but in his daughter's memories of him. Also, I couldn't shake the feeling that he had been hiding something, that this whole thing was deeper, maybe even troublesome, to his reputation. I felt like Antonine had sensed the same thing. *Had he seen what I saw out there? Or more?*

"Man, you've got it bad for this chick," said Bomber suddenly.

He was sitting on the end of the bed, barely visible in the dim light. I hadn't even seen him come in.

"You keep thinking about her and this ghost ship in circles. Why don't you just ask her to be your girlfriend, express your deepest and undying love, and actually *do* something about the phantom boat? What you need for all of this is a solution, man, an actual solution. What a concept, eh?"

"If I try to do that, will you go away?"

"No," he said. "I'm your buddy. I'll never go away."

He got up, walked through the wall and out onto the beach.

"I'll see you later," he said in the distance.

I stared up at the ceiling, listened to the waves crashing against the shores of Chaleur Bay, and focused. I started thinking about the way Antonine had described some of the things that happened the night she and her father chased the ship out onto the water. She had not only spoken of the two of them seeing a woman at the bow of the boat, on fire—and I had seen that too, which was worrisome enough—but Jackson Clay had also observed that flaming figure struggling in the water near a little island. And he had reached down to pull something out of the water.

I sat bolt upright. *He pulled something out of the water?* We had to know what it was...and if he kept it.

THE NEXT MORNING I woke to the sound of Mom and Dad and Bill and Bonnie putting together a big breakfast downstairs. They were also deep into another conversation.

"The real-estate values have just been skyrocketing in this area recently," said Bill in a voice so loud that I could hear every word from my bed. "That's just tremendous. We were wise to set down roots here."

I glanced outside, saw how high in the sky the sun was, and realized I had slept in. It had taken me so long to fall asleep that once I was under, I had gone totally comatose. I had been dreaming, too, that I was out on Chaleur Bay with Antonine and her dad, watching him pull a young woman's corpse from the water.

I got up and padded downstairs, met by the dogs, of course—whom I now knew as Jordy, Joanie, Johnnie, and Georgie—in the hallway. Just as they had done every morning since I had been here, they jumped up on me, shoved their paws into my groin, and slobbered on my hands and all that sort of lovely stuff—behaviour Bonnie thought was hilarious. She let them lie on the couches, too, and woe to anyone who asked them to move over. I could smell meat on their breath from the "special" dog food Bonnie has for them, even though she also feeds them things off the table. The dogs are pretty picky about the table stuff; they want the right sort of meat. Not big vegetarians, these guys.

"I often prefer animals to people," I heard Bonnie saying to Mom, who didn't reply.

Do you mean people such as yourself...or *other* people? I felt like asking, though thankfully I didn't.

The breakfast that was being prepared would not have interested her dogs much. It was somehow heavy on the health food too: fried green tomatoes, more quinoa, bread bought from a local baker, local cheese, organic eggs, and freshly squeezed orange juice. Thank God for the bread and eggs. Bonnie knew more ways to rearrange veggies and quinoa into a meal than anyone on earth.

Bill had started talking about the election again and I was not in the mood to hear it. I decided I had had enough. It was not my id coming out, it was Dylan Maples. It was me.

"I'll tell you about Jim Fiat," announced Bill, "I had a problem with the garbage collection a couple of weeks ago and Jim has been on the local council for a little while—still is, actually, just taking a leave of absence to run for federal member. So, I thought, given all this stuff he says about answering his own phone—he actually has that in his ads, if you can believe it—I thought I would test him. You know, see if his 'A Friend, A Neighbour, Not a Politician, Not an Elite,' stuff had any validity. So, I call him up to straighten out my garbage problem, and Jim Fiat himself answers the phone, right in the middle of his campaign!"

"Yeah," I said, shuffling up to my high stool and surveying the veggies, "smart move on his part."

"Uh," said Bill, "yes, I thought so too. He sounded very concerned."

"Another smart move on his part," I added.

"What do you mean by that?"

"Did he solve your problem?"

"As a matter of fact, he did." Bill looked at Dad with a grin on his face. "Imagine that, everything solved within seconds."

"Not hard to do, when you're an elite," I said.

"Pardon me?"

"Isn't he rich?"

"Uh, yes, I suppose, but he's local."

"He's local and rich, very well connected, an elite, and a politician." I paused. "Don't you think maybe that's how he solved your problem?"

"He is not a politician. He is adamant about that. He is just a guy from around here who cares about real people."

I let the "real people" comment pass and jumped on the other ridiculous thing he had said.

"I thought he was running for election? If he says he is not a politician, then it seems to me that he is lying to you. If I'm a mechanic and I say I'm not really a mechanic, I'm actually your buddy, in order to get you to pay me to fix your car, then I'm lying to you. So let's see what we have here: a rich, privileged guy who is 'against the elites,' and a liar. I think that about sums him up."

There was absolute silence in the room. Mom and Dad both had their mouths open and they were eating. It was not a pretty sight.

"What's so bad about being elite at something anyway?" I continued. "I like watching elite hockey players and I want an elite teacher to teach me in school, an elite doctor to keep me healthy. Don't you?"

"We don't watch hockey," said Bonnie in a very quiet voice. I guess it was the only thing she could come up with. Sometimes she looked a little embarrassed at the things her husband said.

"I think he is answering his own phone," I continued, on a roll, "to get you to think he cares. To get his butt into power so he can put forward whatever plans he has, and he's sucking you in. Think about who this guy is, Bill." I hadn't referred to our esteemed host by his first name yet, but at this point, I didn't care. "Who are his parents, what's he ever done for a living?"

"His father was…was a businessman, in real estate, quite successful," said Bill.

"Ah, yes, a man of the people. How successful?"

"Very. Grew up here, was here for a long time."

"Was? Not here anymore?"

"He…he owns some hotels in Halifax now."

"So, Jim's dad has become a foreigner. When did he move away? I thought Jim has always been a local guy?"

"Well, he was born here, and then went to Halifax with his family. He has come back recently. Has some business ventures in the area, got on city council, as I told you. His father ran for office apparently, too, way back when. In Ottawa for a while, then lost, I've heard."

"Wow, so our Jim is not only a politician who says he isn't a politician, but he is the son of a politician—one who held high office for a while!"

"Dylan, have you tried the fried tomatoes?" asked Mom, who was giving me a really ugly look.

"So," I continued, "I understand why Jim Fiat, the politician who isn't a politician, the elite who is against the elites, might be big on all sorts of local issues, but why does he talk so much about immigration? We studied the levels of government and their powers in school last year and immigration is a federal issue, isn't it?"

"Yes, and he is running for federal office," said Bill, looking really peeved now, saying this as if I were a moron.

"I understand that. It's just that I wonder why it is such a big deal to him, focused as he says he is on local things, on the 'little guy' around here?"

"It is part of his whole brand," said Bill.

"Brand?"

"Well, perhaps I shouldn't put it that way. It is simply part of who he is and what he believes in. He is a family man. You know," added Bill, glancing at Dad, "you see him all the time on the street and on the beach, shaking hands with average people, talking to the fishermen."

"Does he have kids?"

"No, but—"

"Does he plan to? Will he spend all his free time with them...or with his dream of being a big-shot in Ottawa?"

"Dylan, that's enough," said Dad.

I was not in the mood, though, not at all. Not after all Antonine and I had been through, not after Bill barely spoke to her, not after hearing about how her dad was treated in this town.

"I think he—" began Bill.

"Why does Jim care about who comes into this country? Millions of people in the world can barely survive. I'm a kid and I know that. Shouldn't we open our arms to them? Especially given how privileged we are here...how privileged he is."

"If you will let me finish," said Bill testily. He paused. "Jim Fiat believes in family values, local values, whether you accept that or not. He is not 'against immigration,' as you put it. I would not give a man with that sort of racist policy a second of my time. But he believes we have to be smart about who enters Canada. He believes in the 'Canadian Way' and, young man, I do as well. We want people coming here who at least share some of our values. You will understand when you get older."

Ah, yes, that old chestnut.

"Have you ever thought about the possibility that, in some cases, some of the people coming here might have *better* values than some of us?"

Silence again. Then I excused myself. I left the room and went out to the beach without looking back, like a jet fighter who had just strafed the enemy and then flown back up into the sky. Even the dogs didn't seem to want to look at me. That confrontation actually made me feel good, though. It made me feel like I, little old Dylan Maples, had values, and I had stood up for them. The only thing I wasn't feeling very good about was what it was going to be like when I came back to the house later. I quickly stopped myself from worrying about that, though, and put my head into a "live for the moment" kind of mood. It was Saturday, too, perfect for school kids to head to the beach. We were going home on Monday, but I was pretty sure I would find Antonine on the beach at Youghall that very morning.

I almost ran there, thinking about the details I had gone over in my head in bed last night, about she and her father seeing a figure slashing around in the water, and him reaching into the bay and pulling something out.

It was a warm morning and, just as I predicted, there were lots of people on the beach, adults and kids. Young couples were walking around holding hands or tanning together on towels, and little ones were screaming as they ran in and out of the waves. Antonine, however, was not hard to spot. I saw her from a mile away. There was a bonus, too: she was wearing a bathing suit. A black bikini. Man, she looked great.

"Hi!" she called out with a big grin, waving from far away.

She was alone again. I had noticed she had never come to the beach with friends...kind of like the way I was operating these days back home.

"Where's your bathing suit?" she asked, and I wondered, for a second, if she was even more like me than I imagined.

I didn't say anything about the things that were occupying my mind last night. We just goofed around. I rolled up my pant legs and walked with her to the water. We kept doing the same things over and over without getting tired of them. She would splash me, she would move toward a wave, and then it would engulf her and she would scream and come running back out, sometimes grabbing my hand when she did. I think I was happier than I had been in years.

But I needed to talk to her.

Finally, we lay down on her big beach towel.

"You know I have to go in a couple of days, right?" I said. "Not even two full ones."

"I know." She said it quietly, almost sadly, which kind of made me feel good.

"So, if you want to figure out anything more about the ghost ship, about what your father saw, then we need to do that now."

"What else can we figure out? It's like we're at a dead

end with it, just like everyone else who has investigated it. People see it all the time, and in numbers, so there's a moving fire out there, there's no question...but there is absolutely no explanation for it."

I was thinking about what Florence Green had said, about "something in between."

"What my dad saw, though," continued Antonine, "was weird. Weirder than all the rest, and embarrassing. I think we should just leave it alone."

"Not me."

"What?" She looked over at me.

"I think we have to go with the idea that there really is some sort of actual ship out there, even treat the details of what your dad saw—and what I kind of saw—as real."

"You do?"

"Let's consider it all to be absolutely factual from now on. You and your father glimpsed someone in the water near the ship, didn't you? Someone on fire?"

"Yeah. That's what I remember, anyway. But maybe I'm making it up."

"Don't say that. Treat it as real, and examine it again in your memory. You said your dad just left the scene... but that isn't true, is it? He did something."

Antonine paused for a moment. "He pulled something out of the water," she said after a while, her voice quiet, as if she were seeing her father reaching into the bay long ago.

"Yes."

"But maybe I made that up, too."

"No, these are facts, nothing less. Did you see what he had in his hands?"

"Not really. I just remember him pulling it out."

"What did he do with it after that?"

"He put it in our boat, I think. I remember not wanting to look at it. I was terrified."

I had to ask her.

"Was it a body?"

Antonine thought about it for a while.

"I don't think so. Dad would have done something about that. He would have told the authorities. I was with him a lot over the next few days, I remember that, and he wasn't away much or doing anything suspicious. I think, even as a kid I would have sensed that. You know, him slipping away to...bury something." I could see her swallow.

"So, whatever he had, he may have kept close by."

"Yeah, maybe," she nodded. "Anybody else would have rushed to the local paper with it too, but not Dad. Like I keep telling you, he was worried about his reputation and would not have wanted to seem like he was in any way unstable."

"Where would he put something—not a body—that he wanted to keep close by so no one else could find it?

Antonine thought for a moment again. Then her eyes widened.

"He...he had one place where he kept things, where no one else went. I told you about it." She looked out toward the water. "I...I remember, when he was dying, he said to me: 'little one, you know where I keep my treasures, don't you?' I forget exactly what he was talking about, but I recall that he gave me a longing look, as if he wanted to say more. Treasures! That's what he called the tools and other things he kept in his shed in the backyard."

I remembered seeing that little building, sitting there on their lawn like an off-limits shrine.

"Let's go!" I said.

14

TREASURE

We didn't walk back into Bathurst, we ran. At least, we started out that way. Man, Antonine could motor. She must have been on the track team or something because I not only found it hard to keep up with her, but I was sucking air in about five minutes and Antonine looked like she was barely breathing. I guess that's what happens when you give up hockey.

At the end of Youghall Drive where it meets busy St. Peter Avenue, which brings you into town, we caught a bus and took it almost to the end of her street. Then, we realized we had a problem: her mom was home, the little car parked in the driveway. We cut across the neighbour's lawn in order to keep out of view and then sneaked around to the rear of the house. Antonine and I got onto our hands and knees and scurried across the backyard, hiding in the playground equipment, until we got to the shed.

"I don't think anyone has been in here for a long time," she whispered.

It actually didn't make any sense to be that quiet since her mom wouldn't be able to hear us from inside the house if we just spoke in normal voices. Antonine reached up, turned the doorknob, and we went inside.

There was a large work table at the far end of the shed with a vice grip and a power saw on it, and some tools arranged neatly on top. Other tools were hanging from hooks on the walls, and there were stacks of lumber piled up on the floor. It had the fragrance of wood and work.

Antonine breathed deeply. "It smells like Dad," she said.

"He used the word 'treasure,'" I said, "could that mean something other than just his tools?"

As I said it, my eyes rested on a big wooden chest, like a container for a pirate's stash, on the floor in the corner next to the table. When I turned to Antonine, I noticed she was looking at it too.

"In there!" she said.

There was a lock on it, though, a thick one. I looked around the room and found a pair of huge bolt cutters hanging from the wall. I retrieved them and applied them to the lock, squeezing as hard as I could. I couldn't even make a dent. Then I felt Antonine pressing herself up against me and gripping the handles on the bolt cutters too. We squeezed together and the business ends of the big tool started making a mark, then cut through a bit, then a bit more…and finally the lock snapped off!

We both just stared at it for a minute.

"You do it," I finally said.

We dropped the cutters to the floor and she knelt down in front of the chest. She hesitated, and then pulled off the lock. I noticed her hands were shaking.

Then she opened the lid.

There was just a bunch of wood inside. Disappointing. Antonine started going through it, almost as if she had nothing better to do at this point, lifting out sticks and planks, dropping them on the floor. Then she stopped.

"What's this?"

It was big, stretching almost the full length of the two-metre-long chest, and about half a metre across, left there at the bottom, hidden under the other pieces of wood. That wasn't the only thing that was unusual about it. Three quarters of it was black.

Antonine reached down and picked it out. Some of the black came off on her hands.

"It's been burned," I said.

"A burned piece of timber hidden in a treasure chest," said Antonine.

We looked at each other.

"This wood isn't from around here," she said, running her hands along the unburned part to feel the grain. There was still some bark on the sides, unusual-looking, grey with ridges in it.

"How would you know that?"

"My Dad taught me all about wood, about the grains, the way it looks after it is sawed, and about different barks. Even though he was American, he took a great deal of pride in the forests we have around New Brunswick, and the lumber we produce. He and I used to walk in the woods and he would point things out and make me identify trees." She looked down at the plank. "I have never seen anything like this before."

"What does this mean?"

There was a noise in the backyard. Someone was approaching. Thankfully Antonine had closed the shed door. The sound of footsteps striding through the grass drew closer. Then we saw the doorknob turn. Antonine dropped the burned piece of wood into the chest and slammed down the lid.

"Antonine?"

The door opened and someone entered. It was Eve.

"I thought I heard someone in here. What are you doing, no one ever—" Then she noticed me, standing very close to her daughter. "Oh," she said and a little smile grew on her face.

"No," said Antonine, "no, it isn't what you think."

"And what do I think?"

"Uh…you know…it…it isn't that."

"Then what is it, mademoiselle?"

"Uh…" I said, "I'm interested in woodwork. Antonine said she would show me around Mr. Clay's shed. It…it's amazing!"

"'Show you around?'" asked Eve. "This gigantic room? How long does the tour take?"

Two people stretching their arms out together could almost touch opposing walls. Eve smiled again.

"Why don't you two come in and have something to eat? I've baked cranberry muffins and I'll make some hot chocolate."

She was very nice about it. Once we were inside, she didn't ask us a single uncomfortable question, though I did notice that she concentrated on me quite a bit and inquired about my upbringing and if I had any thoughts yet about what I'd like to do for a living.

I knew exactly what Antonine was thinking because I was thinking the same thing. And it had nothing to do with her mother's questions. Was the burned piece of wood from the ghost ship? Was it hold-in-your-hand evidence that this legendary phantom ship actually existed?

Eve kept us at the table for a long time, which I didn't really mind, since the cranberry muffins were insanely delicious and I had about twelve of them, well, not twelve but maybe…seven. Eve looked at me as if I were a Martian as she saw the muffins disappearing down my gullet by the boatload, but she kept offering them to me so what was I supposed to do? Refuse?

Antonine looked ticked off. I think it was because I wasn't supposed to be enjoying myself at this point. We were onto something and we needed to discuss it.

"Dylan needs to go," she finally said. "Your mom said you were to be back by six."

I had just snagged another muffin and almost had it in my mouth. My lips were basically reaching out for it when she spoke. It was just inches away.

"She did?" I said.

"Yes," said Antonine. "Don't you remember?"

"Uh…" I said and gazed at the muffin.

"You can eat that one," said Eve, reassuringly.

I popped half of it into my mouth. It gave me time to chew, and think.

"Yes," I finally said, after my second swallow, "I remember now. Yes, six o'clock." I looked up at their big kitchen clock. "My, it is getting late."

"I'll drive you," said Eve, getting to her feet.

"No!" said Antonine.

"No?"

"I mean," said Antonine, "he wants to walk some of the way. He loves the scenery around here…don't you Dylan?"

I was staring at the one remaining muffin. If I had eaten seven…or eight…then they must have only eaten two each, at the most.

"Yes," I said.

"Do you want to take that one with you?" asked Eve.

"Yes," I repeated.

"I'll be back soon, Mom," said Antonine as she almost lifted me out of my seat and directed me toward the door.

We didn't start talking until we were well down the street. Even then, we didn't talk loudly. It was as if we were involved in some sort of espionage and had to be secretive.

"So, what do we do next?" I asked. We had found an incredible clue and yet we seemed to be at a dead end at the same time.

"Learn more about the wood?"

"Confirm that it came from a ship, and then figure out the age of the ship, maybe?"

"Who would know that? A pirate? One from the sixteenth century?"

We walked along for quite a while before either of us said anything more.

"It didn't really look like a ship timber to me," said Antonine finally.

"Then what is it? Why would your father hide a half-burned piece of wood in his shed?"

"We both know why," said Antonine. She stopped and sighed. "Somehow, it's from the phantom ship."

She said it very quietly, but I had no problem hearing her. I couldn't look at her and the main reason was that I agreed. It was as if we were saying that we'd just found Harry Potter's wand...or Long John Silver's wooden leg.

We had come to King Avenue. I think every town in Canada has either a King or a Queen street. This one ran right through the centre of town and there were many bus stops on it. There was a bus approaching. I'd have to hop on it, if I wanted to get home before it got too late.

"What about Florence Green?" I asked as the driver noticed us waiting and signalled to pull over.

"I don't see her as a former pirate."

"Yeah, but maybe she knows somebody who knows about old ships. She works at the museum, doesn't she?"

I got on the bus, leaving Antonine standing there. I walked back to the rear seats and watched her as we pulled away. She was still in the same spot. She was nodding.

15

EXPERT ANALYSIS

Someone was calling my name. It sounded like Bomber. Then I realized where we were: in a rowboat out on Chaleur Bay, and Antonine was with us. I was wearing her invisible necklace and she was sitting beside me, not saying anything, just smiling at Bomb and me as we talked. He was rowing the boat and in the distance behind him, in the direction we were going, you could see a big ball of fire on the water.

"Dylan!" said Bomber.

"Yeah?"

"You know what I think, pea-brain?"

"What, useless excuse for a human being?"

We always talk this way. It's a form of affection. Trust me.

"D'you know what my greatest moment was?"

"The time you peed your pants at Boy Scouts?"

"Close." He paused. "Be serious for a second. It's important, once you're dead, to remember what is of value in life."

"You aren't dead. Don't be a fart."

"Yeah, I'm dead, Dylan. Answer the question and be serious."

"I don't know, maybe the time you scored four goals in the bantam championship game?"

"No."

"Okay, how about when you came fifth in our class...grade three?"

"No, try again, numb nuts."

"When Lisa Greenway gave you that Valentine?"

Antonine laughed.

"Very good guess, but wrong-o."

"Okay, tell me."

"Remember that time you had that concussion, when you hit your head on the rock going down the hill behind our house on the toboggan, and you almost bought it? Remember, they took you to SickKids Hospital and you were unconscious for, like, half the afternoon and then you slept for long periods after that?"

"Yeah."

"I came in and sat beside you for hours. I even held your hand once or twice and said some prayers."

"How could that be your greatest moment? I didn't even know you were there."

"That's why."

"I don't get it. You might as well have been invisible."

"Well, that's what matters, Dylan. Invisible things. When life is all over, you'll know that."

The ball of fire was suddenly very close.

"Let's go!" cried Antonine, and she and Bomb jumped out of the boat and swam toward the fire. I could see now that it was a ship, an ancient pirate ship, engulfed in flames. There was a woman at the front shrieking in pain, and you could hear men on deck screaming.

"NO!" I yelled after my friends.

I couldn't move, though. I was frozen in place, watching them. They climbed onto the ship! They were both going to die.

"DYLAN!"

I came wide awake. It was Mom, standing over my bed in the very early sunshine, in Bill and Bonnie's house in New Brunswick.

"What?" I groaned.

"There is someone on the phone for you."

I glanced at the digital clock on the bedside table. 7:45 A.M. Sunday.

"Someone?"

"You know who."

"DYLAN?" SAID ANTONINE OVER the phone from her place, sounding very awake.

"Yeah. Do you know what time it—"

"Florence Green is an early riser, gets up at five every morning to go for a jog. I called the museum last night and she wasn't in, but then Mom said I could probably reach her around seven, between her jog and before she headed out to help set up for services at her church."

"Why are you telling me this?"

"She knows someone."

"So do I, in fact. I know many people."

"An old ship expert, dummy."

I brightened. "Really?"

"Yeah, a fisherman named Alfonse Gallant. Lives down near Caraquet."

"Caraquet!" I said loudly and then lowered my voice. Mom had gone back to bed, but it was possible that either of the parental units or the Bill and Bonnie Show were awake enough to hear me.

"I know; it's a long way."

"How are we going to get there?"

"Mom will drive us."

"But—"

"I told her everything. We had a long talk. We were up almost all night. She was really good about it. She is fine with driving us and very interested, though she says it is still our deal. She will just wait in the car. We'll pick you up in about fifteen minutes."

"But—"

She hung up.

I had to get ready. I had no choice.

MOM WASN'T MY BIGGEST fan after the way I'd talked to Bill yesterday, but she let me go anyway. Maybe she wanted to be rid of me for a while.

The Clays arrived in about fourteen minutes. I don't even know how they did it, since I thought it would take much longer than that. They didn't look like they hadn't slept at all. They were both excited, their hair combed and shining, and they were chatting away. That is another thing about females: it seems they can just crawl out of bed and look like a million bucks. We, on the other hand, look like something the dog dragged in until we've had a good breakfast and maybe a lounge or two on the couch.

Eve had actually brought breakfast for me! It was some sort of omelette wrap and it was pretty awesome. Well, it wasn't just one wrap…it was three of them. Eve had seen my appetite.

The first thing that surprised me when I got into the car, though, wasn't the big bag of great-smelling wraps Eve deposited on my lap as I crammed myself into the back seat, it was the fact that there was a third passenger—and that occupant took up more room than the three of us put together. It was the burned ship timber, stuck between the two front seats and extending all the way back to the rear windshield, almost touching it. The black part was right next to my head.

We cut back through Bathurst, right across town and East Bathurst and then along the same route that I had been on with the parental units and the Bill and Bonnie Show. We went by Salmon Beach again and past the houses sparsely placed in the beautiful countryside and the little Acadian villages, the blue water evident from the road. Neither Antonine nor Eve said much and that was fine with me. We had too many things on our minds. I just wanted to look out the window, out over the bay, and imagine what this guy might tell us. It was all made more intense by the ship timber being right there next to my nose. It isn't every day that you hang out with a piece of lumber from a ghost ship.

Alfonse Gallant lived on the Bathurst side of Caraquet, just before you turned to head toward the Acadian Historic Village, in that little place called Grande-Anse that Bill had pronounced so inappropriately. Well, Monsieur Gallant didn't actually live in the village, he was out on the water. We passed the Marché Grande-Anse and then turned left at a big church, Catholic I'm guessing, like almost all the other ones around here, and headed toward the water. It was beautiful. The houses weren't big or fancy for the most part, not like Bill and Bonnie's, but they were very well kept, as if their owners took a lot of pride in their homes and community. It almost seemed as if we were going to drive right into the water for a while. The land and the road sloped downward, and we could see a little man-made harbour like a U in the water and boats lined up there at a wide-plank dock.

"This man spent his entire life fishing these waters," said Eve from the driver's seat.

Alfonse's house looked lonely, sitting on its own at the far end of the road, just a small building almost like a trailer but with a fresh coat of blue paint on it and lovely flower beds everywhere. I noticed the paint was almost exactly the colour of the bay. There was some sort of turret rising up from one side, like a miniature lighthouse. Eve pulled up into the Gallants' gravel driveway.

"If this visit doesn't tell you what you need to know, then I don't know what will. Alfonse knows the bay like no one else and has an encyclopedic knowledge of the marine history of the area. It seems he knows every boat that ever sailed here, right back to the sixteenth century." She smiled. "Now, out you get, you two. I'm going in to Caraquet for some groceries. I'll see you in half an hour."

We wrestled the wood out of the car and made our way up to the front door, but we didn't have to knock. Madame Gallant, a smiling, rotund woman under five feet tall, wearing a lovely bright dress that I doubted she normally wore around the house, opened the screen door just as we stepped onto the front porch.

"Bienvenue à Acadie!" she said to me.

"Merci beaucoup," I managed, which made her giggle.

We were very excited, and it probably showed, imagining what Alfonse was going to tell us.

The greeting inside, however, was not nearly as friendly.

"No!" shouted Alfonse Gallant the instant he saw us.

We had just stepped into the house, both of us gripping the plank, turning to our left and looking down the long narrow living room with a big window that gave an incredible view of the bay, toward a white-bearded man in jeans and suspenders and a red plaid shirt. He had been sitting in an easy chair reading but had looked up to see us when we entered. He didn't just shout "No!" He also waved his hand at us in a dismissive way, as if to say to us "get out of my house!"

"Alfonse!" cried Madame Gallant.

After showing us in, she had immediately gone to her kitchen table to retrieve a big tray, on which were arranged two cups of tea and two tall glasses of juice along with a selection of some of the best-looking oatmeal-raisin cookies I'd ever laid eyes on, not to mention an entire plate of raspberry tarts. Man, it looked awesome. I had somehow noticed it with my well-trained peripheral vision. On the ice, I was known for being a good passer. Bomb was always my favourite target. My teammates used to say that I could spot him out of the side or the back of my head at full speed. I had to say, though, locating these raspberry tarts was at least as impressive, especially with an old man yelling at you to get the heck out of his house.

Madame Gallant started really giving it to him in French. She dressed him up and down and sideways and his face started to fall. He looked quite guilty. Then he said something to her that sounded like a sort of apology.

She turned to us and motioned toward the couch and the other living room chairs. They all looked very comfortable and every last one had a great view through the picture window at the water.

"Assiez-vous," she said to us. That meant "sit down." I at least knew that from French class.

Antonine and I seated ourselves next to each other with the board across our knees.

"Monsieur Gallant," Madame Gallant said to us in heavily accented French, "'az sometheeng to say to you." She gave him a stern look.

"I am sorry, please accept my apologies," he said to us in clear English. "I was not referring to you. You are most welcome in our home."

Madame Gallant glowed at him, and then at us, and then motioned toward the food.

"Bon appetit!"

Well, I didn't need any more encouragement. I got my mitts on a tart first and was shocked to find that I had another one in my hand before I had even finished the first one. I felt like such an animal, such an impolite Anglo boob, but something had just come over me. These tarts were delicious in a way that was almost unfair.

"These are the best tarts I've ever tasted," I managed to say.

Madame Gallant glowed again. She pushed a cookie my way.

"I..." stammered Alfonse, "I was referring to what you are carrying. That was what I was saying no to."

"Monsieur Gallant," added Madame Gallant, "feels very, uh, strongly, about ships."

"And that is not from a ship!" he snapped. "I could tell that from across the room."

"Then what is it?" I asked, blurting out what was in my head again.

"I have no idea, but a plank from a ship or a boat of any sort was never that kind of wood, that length, that thickness, sawed that way. It looks more like it came from a house."

"I beg your pardon?" said Antonine.

"A house," he repeated.

"A house?" I mouthed at Antonine.

"Follow me," said Alfonse.

He got to his feet and led us to a little hallway, hobbling a bit as he went. There was a bathroom at the end of it and a bedroom to our left, but he entered another room on his right. Nearly every inch of the wall had either a painting or a photograph of a ship or a fishing boat and there were stacks of books about marine topics piled nearly to the ceiling in every inch of the room. Models of ocean-going vessels sat on top of them and on shelves, some of them ships in bottles. He motioned us over to a desk. There, he started thumbing through a pile of papers, all of them almost the length of the desk. I noticed that one of his thumbs was missing. He saw me staring at it.

"Gave that one to the sea," he said. "Now, look here."

He fished out about a half dozen of the papers and laid them on the desk in front of us.

"Portuguese, 1500."

We looked down and saw an ancient ship, meticulously drawn, as if x-rayed, all its masts, its decks, its innards on display in a sort of three-dimensional rendering. He pulled it back and showed us the next one.

"Spanish, 1600." He displayed two more. "English, 1750 and French, 1750."

Then he somehow spread them all out so we could look at the whole group at once, and jabbed at the cross-sections.

"See the planks used on these? Do they look anything like your board? Not a drop!"

He suddenly seized the entire desk and wrenched it back from the wall and sideways, the legs grinding on the floor.

"Look down," he said.

We glanced downward and saw a long piece of wood there, weathered and brown but smooth as concrete and about twice the width of our board and twice as long. It went nearly the entire length of the room.

"That's a piece out of an English man-of-war from the Battle of Restigouche. Don't ask me how it is in my possession...because if I told you, I'd have to kill you."

There was silence for a moment. Then he laughed, thank God, bringing his stumped thumb up to cover his mouth.

"But as you see, your piece is nothing like this. It is no more a plank of a ship from those days than it is a part of a spacecraft. I get so many people coming here showing me things like this that are not authentic. I'm sorry, but I lose my patience sometimes. When Eve said it had something to do with the ghost ship, I became a little excited. There was some disappointment, you see."

"You mentioned our wood looked as if it was from a house," I said.

"That's what it seems like to me. Someone is trying to fool you."

Antonine frowned.

"It is curious, though," Alfonse continued, "that it is partially burned."

After that, we returned to the living room and had a lovely chat with the Gallants about Acadia and fishing, and Alfonse and I even got in a few jabs about his dreadful Montreal Canadiens and my magnificent Leafs, but he refused to say another word about the plank.

"WE DIDN'T LEARN A single thing," Antonine told her mother as we piled back into the car, jamming the piece of wood into place again.

"Or maybe we did," I said. "We can now be absolutely certain that we are out of our minds. This is just some chunk of burned wood that Mr. Clay kept in his work shed."

"Why would he do that?" asked Eve.

"Why would he keep it at the bottom of a chest if he wasn't hiding it?" added Antonine.

"I don't know," I said, "maybe that just happened to be where it ended up."

"Hiding it or not," said Eve, "there is a reason why he would hang on to something like this. I know my man. Jackson wasn't a pack rat. You likely noticed how tidy things were in his shed."

"What are you saying?" asked Antonine.

"I'm saying I believe my husband and both of you. Old Man Gallant must be wrong. Maybe there is an old ship—a single ship, a special one—that he knows nothing about. This piece of wood came from that ghost ship. You just have to prove it."

"Oh, that'll be easy!" I snapped. Wow, I had actually done the id thing with Mrs. Clay.

She laughed. "You've got that right."

THE OTHER PROBLEM WE had, of course, was that we were running out of time. Mom, Dad, and I were heading home tomorrow.

We stopped at Antonine's house so we could get the wood out of the car and back into the shed and Eve could drop off her groceries. It seemed strange, in a way, to be keeping a piece of burnt wood, but the thought of throwing it out never crossed our minds, nor was there even the slightest inclination to toss it outside somewhere in the backyard. We maneuvered it out of the seats and carried it across the lawn as if it were a vase of Ming china, or a coffin.

When we got it back into the shed, we set in on Mr. Clay's workbench and examined it closely for a while, our eyes about six inches from its surface, looking it up and down and turning it over several times. I think we were hoping to find obscured initials or a date or something like that, but we found nothing for a long while. Antonine started running her hands along its surface, just feeling for a clue, I suppose.

"Here!" she suddenly exclaimed.

"What?"

"There's a hole here and another one here, both at the end of the board. Feel it."

She took my hand. I'm not sure she had to do that in order for me to discover what she was getting at, but I didn't mind, let me tell you. I just loved the feel of her hands, so much so that for a few seconds I didn't even notice what she was pressing my fingers down onto.

"Can you feel it?"

"Eh?"

"Can you feel it?"

"Oh, yeah."

"Two holes, right?"

"Yeah," I finally said, getting my hand to feel the board instead of her hand.

"What does that mean?"

"Nail holes."

"Right. Someone nailed this board to something."

"But these holes are awfully small. This is from a big, ocean-going pirate ship from hundreds of years ago and it has two tiny nail holes in it? Monsieur Gallant must be right."

"Maybe they used smaller nails then?"

"I doubt it. From what I know from history class, nails were bigger in the old days, if anything, usually thick and square at the head. They would leave a large, square indentation. Also, if someone were just using little nails, you'd think he or she would use a whole bunch of them to keep this craft together on the ocean waves."

Antonine just nodded her head, deep in thought.

"This doesn't make any sense," she finally said, "none of it does." She sighed. "There isn't a single thing that we've discovered that means anything or connects to anything else, or fits my father's story or the legend! Nothing! Not from him hiding a burnt piece of wood in the shed, to it being a weird kind of wood, to Monsieur Gallant saying it never could have been used for a ship, to these tiny friggin' little nail holes!"

Her voice had risen in frustration. She shoved the board and it flew off the work table and crashed down onto the floor. I could see tears welling in her eyes. This was a connection to her dad—maybe her last one—a connection that meant a great deal to her, and had to do with something she and he did together a long time ago. It was something that he had felt bad about, that had haunted him, something that made him seem like he was out of his mind, and here she was, getting nowhere with it. It was slipping from her grasp just the way he had...the way Bomb had from me.

I put my arm around her.

Wow, that was unbelievable. I do not understand how I was able to summon what I needed to actually do that—put my arm around a girl, and *this* girl.

Then something else happened that just about blew my mind. She turned and hugged me. Now, I know she did that the other time, on the beach, when we were cold. This, however, had nothing to do with being cold. It was precisely the opposite. She felt different this time, smaller and more fragile, pressing in to me as if she needed me. It made me feel like a guy...not that I am not a guy, but it made me feel that way. I have never felt anything like that before in my life.

"Antonine!" Eve was calling from the house. "I've made a snack!"

Wow, now there was a tough choice. Food...or Antonine.

"We better go," she said quietly.

16

THE BIG HOUSE ON THE BEACH

A snack. That was what Antonine's mom had said. As we exited the shed, though, I had visions of grandeur. From what I had seen of her previous work, Eve Clay's idea of a snack was more like a smorgasbord of delights to my nearly-sixteen-year-old-boy brain. Not that I was entirely forgetting about what I had left behind— Antonine in my arms—but I headed toward the house nicely focused on the task before me: the destruction of the so-called snack. I actually beat Antonine to the back door. I think I was in the kitchen before she even hit the hallway. And there it was: some kind of drink in two tall tumblers and two plates with big sandwiches on them that looked like BLTs, and another plate with what appeared to me to be homemade chocolate chip cookies.

Then Antonine said something absolutely bizarre.

"I'm not hungry."

"What?" I said.

"I can't eat anything right now."

"You can't?" I glanced at the food. "Really?"

"No, I'm kind of depressed. I'd rather go to the beach or something, go for a walk, talk about all of this some more."

"Talk?" I said.

"Oh, honey," said Eve and took Antonine into her arms.

Okay, so now I wasn't going to get anything to eat and her mother was hugging her, not me. That seemed like a sort of lose-lose situation. What was this, a girl thing? You don't want to eat and you opt for talking instead? A stroll on the beach? Feelings?

Then Eve, a smart woman who seemed to know what guys were all about, came to the rescue.

"I'll take you two to the beach, and I'll wrap up a sandwich for you, Dylan, and throw in a couple of cookies too."

"Going to the beach is an excellent idea," I said. "We indeed need to talk about this. Let's go."

Antonine gave me a bit of a look.

SHE DIDN'T TAKE ANY food with her, which really blew me away, and she actually didn't talk much, at least for the first little while we were there. Since it was a Sunday, there were mobs of people on Youghall Beach. Eve dropped us off in the parking lot and we hit the busiest area first, and then started to walk along the water in the direction of Bill and Bonnie's place, and the bigger houses. When we were about halfway there, Antonine sat down on a large rock near the grass and I sat with her. She was looking out over the bay again, just as she was doing when I first met her. We could barely see the little island out there, to our left, up the coast a bit, the one that Jackson Clay said he and his little daughter were near as the burning ghost ship of Chaleur Bay really began to rage. I wasn't looking at Antonine, but I could see, with my amazing peripheral vision, that she was deep in thought.

"If we are going to take this board seriously as evidence of a ghost ship, then shouldn't the part of it that isn't burned be in worse shape than it is?" she finally said.

"What do you mean?"

"If it's a few centuries old, shouldn't it be deteriorating more?"

An image of the board lying there on the work table back in Jackson Clay's shed came into my mind. I examined the surface again. She was right. It looked old, but not *really* old. I thought again of the tiny nail holes. Something about all of it, when considered together, made the hairs on the back of my neck stand on end.

"What if it really is from the ghost ship...and it's new?" I said. "At least, a relatively new piece of wood."

We looked at each other. I could see in her eyes that this possibility meant something to her too.

"How could that be?" she said in a whisper.

I almost didn't want to say the next thing that occurred to me, but we were trying to get to the truth about this, so I just blurted it out.

"Your father would have known that. He would have known it was new. He would have known it immediately."

"Yeah."

"That would have freaked him out. He pulled a fresh piece of wood off an ancient ghost ship?"

"This is freaking me out."

"Maybe that was another reason he was not investigating things. He knew this was beyond strange. Something wasn't right about it even for a ghost ship. Maybe he felt guilty that—" I stopped.

"—he did nothing about it," finished Antonine. "He was closer to the ship than anyone had ever been, he saw a young woman on fire, he had a piece of timber that had come right out of time as if it were just cut from a tree, and he said and did nothing about any of it!"

She got up and started walking briskly along the beach. I struggled to keep up. We were nearing Bill and Bonnie's house.

"You have to put yourself in his shoes," I said to her, breathless. "It was like you said, he was a black man and he didn't want to seem like a lunatic, he couldn't afford that. It wasn't his fault; it was the fault of every person who made him feel that way. It is the fault of everyone who has ever made anyone feel that way. He couldn't do a single thing about this. He really couldn't. You and I wouldn't have done any different. Antonine, he protected your reputation."

"I think about him so often, Dylan. All the time." She sounded like she was crying.

"I think about Bomb, too."

She slowed down. We were within sight of the big back deck at Bill and Bonnie's place. I could see four people sitting out there on the lawn chairs—our hosts and my parents. They weren't facing our direction. I could see Bill popping one of his pairs of glasses on and then the other, glancing up and down at an article he was reading and talking to Dad about. I looked at the sand and just kept walking. Antonine didn't seem to realize exactly where we were.

"Dylan?" I heard Mom call out.

How does she do that? She'd had her back to me for God's sake! Talk about peripheral vision. Mothers are awesome in that department. I bet they would be able to spot a teammate in the open on the ice better than Connor McDavid. Although, the player in the open would have to be one of their kids.

"Hello, Mother," I said and kept walking. *Mother?* I had never called her that in my life. She looked at me as if I were a Klingon or something and just watched the two of us as we walked past the house and on up the beach toward the even bigger and fancier houses.

"I think your mom is calling you," said Antonine, wiping her eyes.

"Yeah, I know. Just keep walking."

I lifted my chin and looked straight ahead. As I did,

I noticed something in the distance. There was a crowd gathering up there. That was strange because the beach got very narrow in that direction and there wasn't much room for many people, usually they formed a thin line of humanity near the water. Now, however, they were bunching up. It was hard to know why. Something had gotten their attention. My first thought was that the ghost ship had reappeared, though this was not really the right time of day or the right sort of weather, hot and sunny as it was. No one was turned toward the water, either; instead, they were in groups facing inward, as if something or someone moving along the beach was of great interest.

"You're right, there was nothing Dad could have done about it," said Antonine, "but maybe we can do something. Something stinks about this. That board just isn't right. It isn't from around here and it isn't from the past. Was that ship slipping through some sort of hole in time, or was that board—"

"What's going on up there?" I interrupted.

She looked along the beach in front of us. We could both now see that indeed someone had nearly everyone's attention up there. I could tell it was a man. He was wearing a suit, too, which struck me as rather strange beach attire. He was shaking hands with people and they seemed anxious to greet him.

We moved closer.

"It's Jim Fiat," said Antonine. "He lives just over there." She pointed to a huge house about four or five houses away. It towered over the two on each side of it. "I remember the Fiats building it when I was a kid."

Ah, yes, I thought, Bill's wonderful "man of the people," his "enemy of the elites," come down from his castle to move among the little folks...in his suit, now.

"Mom told me a story once," continued Antonine, "about Fiat's father letting him be a supervisor of some sort during the construction of the house, even though he was only in his late teens. Getting him ready for a business career, I guess."

"I want to meet him this time," I said, and made a beeline for a hive of his well-wishers. "I've got some questions for him."

As I approached, I got a better view of Jim Fiat than I had at the historic village. He was a heavy-set man, with blond (almost orange) hair that looked dyed to me, a deep perfect tan, and his black suit and bright yellow tie glistened in the sun, obviously purchased somewhere far from this little town in New Brunswick. He was handing out something.

"My personal cellphone number is on these cards!" I heard him say. "You can call me anytime, on my direct line. I will not be living in an ivory tower after you elect me and I get to Ottawa. You can drop by and see me any time!"

I forced my way farther through the crowd and heard some comments from onlookers.

"Go get 'em, Jim!" shouted one man.

"Speak for us," said another lady.

"Run 'er like a business!" cried someone else. "Don't waste our money!"

I wondered who "us" was. Most of these folks were white middle-class or higher-than-that people who didn't really look like they needed anyone speaking for them.

"Glad to represent you," said Jim in a loud voice. "Remember to get out to vote on the thirteenth. Let's put the elites where they are meant to be: on the sidelines!"

There was actually a round of applause.

"I will get jobs for our own folks," continued Fiat, "not people coming in from all over the place, not people who will do any old job and grab up what is available. I do not have anything against outsiders, let me be clear, but we have to look after our own first."

There was another smattering of applause.

"Mr. Fiat!" I called.

Antonine somehow made her way through the crowd, too, and was right next to me. I could feel her shoulder touching mine.

"Yes?" he said and took my hand the instant I spoke. I hadn't really offered my own hand, I'd just brought it up instinctively and he'd seized it. He gripped it as if he were my long-lost friend. Then he looked at me. "How old are you?" he asked.

"I'm almost sixteen."

He dropped my hand.

"Are you from around here?" he asked.

"No, I'm from Toronto."

He smirked. "Ah, we have a man from Bay Street among us! Where the elites make the decisions that affect all of us," he said loudly.

"I'm...a kid."

"No offense, my friend, but I'd rather talk to the real people."

A few spectators cheered and he glanced at Antonine, looked her up and down and at her face, and quickly moved on past us, glad-handing others who approached him, making his way up the beach like the lead goose with his flock following. A few people did not join in, though they still gawked at his entourage with interest.

"You're not real," said Antonine to me with a smile.

"Yeah, I'm a ghost, I guess."

I hadn't asked Fiat a single question. How did he do that? He somehow shook my hand, made a point at my expense to gain more praise for himself, and then was gone before I could even say anything of substance. People cheered him for it.

"You see all these houses here," Antonine said, pointing toward the homes lining the beach near us. Every one of them was relatively new or at least renovated, and as large, or larger, than Bill and Bonnie's. "Almost every person who lives in these homes isn't from around here. It is outside money."

We were just a couple of properties from Fiat's place now. I glanced farther up the beach and it appeared to me that his might be the biggest home of them all. Antonine nodded at it.

"He lives among his enemies, I guess."

"Let's get closer."

"I'll bet he has a fence and security."

Sure enough, he did.

We weren't able to get within fifty metres of the Fiats' back door. Even Bill and Bonnie's deck wasn't like that—you could walk right up to theirs and sit down with them and have a brew or two.

We stood there staring at Jim Fiat's house. It was three storeys high and the first-floor wall facing the water looked like it was entirely made of glass.

"When his father was the Member of Parliament here," said Antonine, "people said he resented the fact that he was never made a cabinet minister. He left the area in a bit of a huff after he lost his last election, leaving this house behind as a sort of summer place. Jim and his wife live there now, most of the time. Old Man Fiat is made of millions, and the rumour is that he is rarely even in his Halifax home these days. Apparently he's more often at his place in Toronto, or the one in L.A."

I thought back to Jim Fiat's perfect tan and expensive suit.

"What were you going to ask him?"

"I got into a bit of an argument about him with our hosts, so I just wanted to get some things straightened out, you know, find out where he really stands on a couple of issues."

"You care about that stuff? Maybe you aren't a kid."

"I don't care that much about it. I just think he's a fake." I shrugged. "Do you follow politics?"

"A little, but there aren't many people at my school who want to talk about it. Most of them just don't care.

I have to say, though, there are a lot of things more important than politics."

"I agree. I just wanted to know why he takes some of the weird positions he has. Like, he wants to decrease the number of people coming into Canada. Not because I have concerns about it, but because it seems like such a dumb idea. A selfish one. It seems like the plan of a rich dude who wants to keep what he has, and it's full of fear of things that are different. I have so many friends back home from all over the world. If you believe in Canada, then you believe it's a good place—not perfect, but good—and you want to share what we have with people in need."

Antonine didn't say anything for a while, just looked at me. In some ways, I had kind of echoed what her mom had said about these things. I hadn't intended to, it was just the way I felt.

"I'd vote for you," she finally said.

Wow, that was a good comment.

"I bet your dad wouldn't have voted for Fiat," I said.

"You've got that right."

It seemed like a moment to take her hand. It would have been an awesome move, like the perfect moment in a movie to make things happen between the two of us. Maybe a kiss, too, a long, romantic one that—

"Look at his house," said Antonine. "There's something funny about it." I had brought my hand out of my pocket but instead of moving it toward her, I reached up and scratched my head. Then I looked toward the house again.

"What do you mean?"

"Look at the wood they used."

That was when we both almost fell over onto the sand. The wood in his house was funny, for sure, but not ha-ha (not St. Louis de Ha! Ha!) funny. It was unusual, a colour and a grain that wasn't used on any other house we'd seen as we walked along the beach or strolled through Bathurst.

It was exactly like the board from the ghost ship.

17

ISLAND VISIT

"**R**emember," said Antonine, "that I told you the Fiats built this house when I was a child? When I think of it now, I realize that it was around the time Dad and I saw the burning ship...that very summer!"

Neither of us knew exactly why, but that felt important. I could tell by the look on her face, which I assumed was similar to the one on my own.

"This could mean nearly anything," I said.

"Yeah," she replied. "It could mean that Jim Fiat isn't a human being. He's a pirate from long ago. It could mean that pirates built his house."

We both laughed. It seemed like the only thing to do.

"What do we do next?" I asked. "Go up to man-of-the-people boy and ask him why your father had a piece of wood from his house in his shed? Why your dad found it in Chaleur Bay near a burning ghost ship from a few centuries back?"

"We could do that if we wanted to look like idiots."

"Maybe there is a perfectly good explanation for this."

"Maybe this wood comes from wherever those ancient ships were built?"

"Maybe," I said, "we have to think outside the box. What if this apparition doesn't exist in the way we are assuming?"

"We need more evidence. We are just clutching at straws right now, starting to consider bizarre theories without really knowing anything. We keep coming up with more and more of these weird facts and they don't seem to go together."

We just stood there kind of gawking at each other for a while. Then we turned and started trudging along the beach in the direction the politician and his fans had gone, heading back to Youghall. The swarm was moving away from us in that direction, a perfect place for Fiat to draw an even bigger crowd.

As we strolled along, I looked out toward the water again. I thought about the two of us going out there just a few days ago, that startling night, and of Antonine and her dad there too, long ago. I remembered the riveting details of her story. I turned my head sideways and looked at her, just stared, as we walked. She glanced back and despite her frustration, grinned at me. Then I looked past her. She didn't seem as if she liked that at first, but was more interested when I spoke.

"The island!" I had noticed the little island out on the water over her shoulder, the one they had neared at the key moment in their adventure, when the enflamed girl had fallen into the bay and appeared to struggle in the water.

"What do you mean?" she asked.

"What if the girl made it to the island? That makes sense, doesn't it? What if there is some sort of indication on its terrain that she was there? Didn't your dad say she was struggling in the water, kind of thrashing her way through it? She must have been trying to reach the only bit of land anywhere near her!"

"Uh, Dylan...that only makes sense if we actually believe there was an actual girl on the boat...on the phantom...on fire."

She was frowning at me.

"Okay, so it sounds nuts, but for now let's go with the assumption not only that the ghost ship is real, but that all of the other stuff we are finding and seeing are connected to it. You said yourself that we have all this evidence and we can't put any of it together. So, we need to find some links, or at least find more evidence that may create a link. We've run out of things around here. I think we need to go back out onto the water and explore that island."

FIRST, WE NEEDED TO borrow another boat. Well steal it, sort of, for a while. Antonine and her mom certainly didn't have enough money to own a boat. Jim Fiat likely had a yacht. I really wished that I knew where it was so we could take it for a spin. Instead, we had to get Antonine to jig another boat down at the docks at Youghall. In order to do that, we had to stick around until it got a bit darker, until the beach began to clear off. Fortunately it was well into September. The sun would be setting soon and the air would cool rapidly.

We borrowed someone's phone, called Eve, told her Antonine would be home late, and not to wait up. Then we did the same thing with my mom. The Bill and Bonnie Show went to bed early, so the parental units had no choice but to hit the hay at the same time.

I bought Antonine a hot dog, chivalrous dude that I am, and was surprised at how much mustard she put on it, though maybe I shouldn't have been. It just kind of made sense, when I thought about it. She was a mustard kind of girl.

We slipped over to the docks side of the beach as the crowd began to thin, and Antonine found the same boat she had taken the other night. She started it up and I jumped in with her. We headed out without looking back, perhaps because we did not want to face seeing someone running toward the shore screaming at us that we had stolen his or her boat. However, there wasn't a sound on the now-still water, just the hum of our vessel's motor as we made a wide turn and swept across the cove and then out into the bay, our wake a question mark on the surface.

I couldn't believe how quiet the world seemed beyond our little boat. I sat beside Antonine, our legs touching, the approaching dusk creating a grey-blue colour in both the sky and the water and making the whole setting seem like something from a different reality. I could imagine a pirate ship out here, its boards not having aged a day, its young crew in the midst of the fire that was raging all around them.

The island was so small that you had to focus to get a bearing on it. We buzzed toward it for a good ten minutes or so and then Antonine cut the motor.

We drifted closer. The near night was eerie here, made especially that way by my memory of seeing the burning ship so close to this spot and knowing Antonine was remembering it too. I tried not to think of the flaming ghost on the water, or of the woman I thought I had seen screaming at its helm. We floated silently forward.

Before long, we bounced against land, a soggy short shoreline that seemed almost to give way as we stepped out and put our feet upon it. We dragged the little motorboat up onto land and between some trees so it couldn't dislodge and drift away on the water. Everything was stunted in size here, the trees more like bushes or Christmas trees for a small apartment. We walked through a stand of mini evergreens, our heads about even with their tops, and before long, the centre of the island opened up into a little clearing. We had only taken about ten or fifteen steps.

We saw it at the same time.

There was another, smaller open area just beyond the clearing. It was on the other side of a row of five scrawny trees that looked like starving castaways. It was about the size of a coffin. We walked up to it. Instinctively, we didn't stand on top it. There, on perhaps the largest tree we had seen, right near the head of the coffin, was what looked like a cross, carved deeply into the bark and right into the tree, grown over now, but its shape still obvious.

We got down on our knees. We looked at each other for a moment and then began to dig with our bare hands. The soil was soft.

I found the first bone. It was only six inches below the surface, obviously put there by someone who had been frantic; someone who did not have the tools or the time for a proper burial. It struck me instantly that it was a human bone, at least it looked like one. It was slender and seemed like part of an arm.

"I think it's a girl," said Antonine quietly.

I wasn't sure why she thought that.

Neither of us could pick it up. We didn't even want to touch it. My hand had pulled back in a reflex when I saw it. And we could tell that there were more bones there, stretched out for about five feet just under the surface. We stood up, shaking, and quickly stepped back from the site, but I put my foot in the wrong place, right near the head of the grave, and I could feel the sole of my running shoe pressing against something round just an inch or two underneath.

A skull.

I lifted my foot as if it had been shocked and actually cried out.

Antonine took my hand and steered me out of the clearing. We quickly made our way down to the boat, got into it and roared out onto the water, heading back toward Youghall Beach, our eyes locked on our destination.

We tied up the boat at the dock, staggered back onto the beach and slumped to the ground.

"So," said Antonine quietly.

"So, there's a body out there on that little island where you and your Dad saw a young girl engulfed in flames floundering toward land...a girl from a ghost ship."

"You ever get the feeling that you don't exist? You ever feel that maybe the whole world is just made up? Maybe I'm just making up everything, even you."

"Yeah," I said. "Lots of times. Scary thoughts." She moved closer to me. "Maybe I made up Bomber too. After all, he's not here anymore."

I could feel tears welling in my eyes. Not a good thing.

She turned to me. "I know I didn't make up my dad. Here is in here." She pointed to her heart. "He isn't just with me, he's inside me. Your friend is inside you, too." She paused. "You know what I think?"

"No." When I looked at her, I could see defiance in her eyes.

"I think my father is more real now than he ever was. I think the spirits of people…the ghosts…are often more real than anything else. It's like Dad said: it isn't the surface of life that matters."

That made me smile. I stood up and she got up with me.

"Does your mom know anyone on the police force?"

"Absolutely."

WHEN WE GOT ONTO the last bus into town, however, sitting at the back far away from the three other folks on board, I started thinking about our situation and a sinking feeling started to come over me.

"We are getting ahead of ourselves," I said. "We're screwed."

Antonine had been sitting there looking excited, our legs touching on purpose this time. She looked at me with a puzzled expression.

"What? What do you mean?"

"They are never going to believe us."

"Dylan, there's a body out there on that island, buried in a shallow grave!" She was trying to keep her voice down. A woman six rows in front of us turned around and looked back.

I lowered my voice even more.

"So what. Sure, they'll go out and examine it, attach it to a missing person's report from long ago, maybe. How are they going to connect this to the phantom though? Or to Jim Fiat?"

"We have the burned plank."

"And a story, told by two kids, about a now-deceased man and his small child seeing a woman on fire on a ghost ship more than a decade ago. That isn't exactly evidence that can be seriously connected to the skeleton on the island, especially evidence that might incriminate one of the most powerful men in this area, about to become the most powerful. I'm sure he has lots of friends on the police force. Imagine us trying to tell them that our burned piece of wood came from his house. They'd laugh us out of the police station. They wouldn't even look at the board."

I could see in Antonine's eyes that she knew I was right. She lowered them, and her head, and stared at the floor below the seat in front of us. All we could hear for a while was the roar of the old bus as the driver changed gears.

"I might as well just get off somewhere and walk back to Bill and Bonnie's."

"No," said Antonine and she took my hand.

All right, I thought, *I'll stay for a while*.

I wondered what she might be thinking. If we couldn't connect all of this to Jim Fiat, if we couldn't come up with some sort of reasonable explanation for what we'd seen out there, her father would still be just a desperate guy who saw a hallucination long ago; who saw someone on fire in a boat and did nothing about it. Antonine would have to live with that forever.

Then I felt her squeezing my hand. When I looked over at her, she was staring back at me and she looked excited. It was as if she was watching something happen in her mind, some sort of possibility.

"I have an idea," she said.

What she then told me was more than a little daring, and dangerous. Her idea could get us both into a boatload of trouble and probably wouldn't even work.

It was all we had, though, and it came from the imagination of one Antonine Marie Clay...so I went along with it.

THE POLICE STATION WAS on King Avenue, just around the corner from the library (though most things are "just around the corner" from almost everything in Bathurst). It was a two-storey brick building with a peaked roof at the entrance, called Le Complex Roussel-O'Neil Complex, a very New-Brunswick name. It was a good-sized building, which made me think that there was a need for a bit of enforcement of the law around these parts. By now, it was late at night so not many police were on duty. In fact, from what we could tell, there was just one available and he looked like he was about ninety years old. We actually had to knock on the bullet-proof glass that went up to the ceiling from the top of the counter a few strides in from the entrance in order to get him to even realize that we were there, that there was life, living species, in the room. It took him about ten minutes to get to his feet and stagger over to us. He was as skinny as a skeleton and his glasses were down near the end of his nose. It looked like he had once filled his uniform much better than he did now.

"Yeah," he wheezed through the little opening.

"We have a crime to report," said Antonine, her voice quavering a bit.

"Eh?" said the man, cupping his hand behind his ear and bending it toward us.

"A crime!" I said.

"A crime? Where?" He looked a little alarmed.

"Out on Youghall Beach."

"Okay," he said and searched around for a pen. He patted his breast pockets and then his pants pockets as we stared at the pen sitting in its holder in front of him. Finally, Antonine tapped at the glass and pointed to it.

"Oh, yes," he said. He seized the pen and began to look for a piece of paper. There was one on the desk, too. He looked around for a while before he noticed it. "Aha!" he said. He poised the pen over the paper. "Description please. Exact location, nature of event, time of event."

"Well," said Antonine. "It hasn't happened yet."

"Pardon me," said the man, "I didn't quite get that. It sounded like you said it hasn't happened yet."

"It hasn't," I confirmed. "Well, the important part has, but that was long ago and not right on the beach...the next part, the part we need the police for at the moment, will happen in a few hours."

He stared at us. His glasses dropped even lower on his nose.

"Is there anyone else here for us to talk to?" asked Antonine. "This might get a little complicated, more than just a report."

"Well," he said, looking relieved, "there is the Forensic Identification Section."

"An entire section is here, at this hour?" I asked.

"Um," he said and cleared his throat, "the Forensic Identification Section, examining dead bodies, you know, that sort of thing is...Constable Gabrielle Leblanc."

"One person?"

"Yes, but she's here! Dedicated lady."

The desk clerk seemed to want to move on from us as soon as possible and immediately summoned Constable Leblanc. A lady I assumed was the officer in question soon appeared.

"Hi Antonine!" she said in a pleasant voice. "How is your mom?"

"She's good, thank you."

Constable Leblanc smiled at her, obviously a fan of Antonine and her mother. She was a slender young woman with long black hair and black eyes, in jeans and a sweater and a short leather jacket rather than a uniform, who only had to hear that we'd found a body to immediately direct us into her office.

There, she began to write down every bit of information we could give her. There were blow-ups of fingerprints and photographs of suspects and gruesome victim images on her walls. Pretty cool. Constable Leblanc got everything out of us, and I mean everything. Antonine tentatively told her in detail about that day long ago when she and her dad saw the ghost ship, and I explained about the half-burned board in Jackson's shed and how that wood matched the material on Jim

Fiat's house, a building that he had been some sort of supervisor on when he was young.

The constable looked more than a little doubtful at the phantom part but we had expected that, and when she heard the last part, about Fiat, it gave her a bit of a pause. She stopped writing and I could see that she was turning something over in her mind.

"When did you and your father encounter the ship... or think you saw it? The exact day."

Antonine didn't know exactly when, but then Gabrielle "Sherlock" Leblanc went to work. She started asking Antonine questions about what time of the year it could have been, when the sun might have been setting, how hot it was, how many people were on the beach, what she remembered doing at about that time, what grade she might have been in, and exactly where her mother was at the time. Slowly, she whittled the mystery down until we had almost an exact date; at least certain of the exact month.

"Just a moment," said Gabrielle, and she turned to her computer. After a while, she looked at us. "I've brought up the information about the Fiat home, when the building permit was issued, when it was actually constructed." She paused for a second. "It was being built the very month you say you saw the ghost ship."

There was silence in the room for a moment.

"So," I finally said, "we have a piece of wood that very likely came from the Fiat home, a home Jim Fiat was involved in building. He may have had some control over the materials and could have covered up for a fair bit of it going missing. We know that those materials were used to make a vessel, which was out on the water during a month when the house was being built. We know that vessel was on fire and we know the piece Mr. Clay acquired was half-burned. We also have witnesses saying there was a young woman on that vessel and that she leapt from it, engulfed in flames and in mortal danger, and tried to swim to the island. We know, too, that the remains of someone, likely a human being, likely young, possibly female, is buried in a shallow grave there."

When I finished, I could feel the goosebumps coming out on my arms and legs. Then Constable Leblanc frowned.

"That is all very compelling, in some ways," she sighed, "but I cannot, in all seriousness, even interview Mr. Fiat about any of this, let alone contemplate arresting him. The evidence against him is circumstantial. We really have no idea what role he played in these events, if any. We will go to the island, exhume the remains immediately and run some tests, but as far as Mr. Fiat's culpability goes…we would need much more than this. Not to mention that he is also one of the wealthiest and most powerful people in our community, in the midst of an election. I simply cannot—"

"Just as we suspected," said Antonine with a smile. "That's perfect."

"Pardon me?"

"You don't need to speak to him," I said. "He wouldn't tell you anything anyway. Why would he? But we have a plan,"

I could feel the nervousness in my voice. We had no idea whether or not Constable Leblanc would go along with this. It wasn't right, really. Thank God she was an admirer of the Clays.

Antonine laid out our plan, and when she was done there was silence in the room.

"Well," said Constable Leblanc, "I know I shouldn't do this. And if this does not transpire as you hope, you will be in some trouble and there may be nothing I can do for you. I will disavow that I agreed to let you do it, too."

"Yes," we both said to her.

"Are you sure?"

"Absolutely," we added.

AN HOUR LATER, AFTER a secret trip to the shed in the Clays'
quiet backyard (Eve must have fallen asleep waiting for
us) and a sneaky visit through my back entrance into
Bill and Bonnie's place, and then into Mom and Dad's
room (they were fast asleep too), Antonine and I got out
of a car about ten houses down Youghall Beach from
Jim Fiat's house on Queen Elizabeth Drive. Two houses
before we reached his, we cut through a walkway and
headed toward the beach.

The night was cool now, the waves gently hitting
the shore, and a big moon sent a glow over the bay.
We walked along the sand in the direction of the huge
house. All the lights were out. When got close, closer
to it than we had ever been before, we realized that the
fence was about seven feet high, more than a foot taller
than we were. We saw the security cameras pointing
toward us, rotating.

"Let's do this," said Antonine.

We threw the board over first and then began to
climb the fence. By the time both of us were on the other
side, the alarm was screaming.

18

MAN OF THE PEOPLE

We climbed the wide wood steps that went up to the elevated deck, the alarm still making a terrible racket. We had been able to see the way the chairs and sofas were arranged on the deck from the beach, so we sat on the ones we had planned to occupy, facing the big picture window. It indeed seemed that Fiat's whole wall facing the beach was window, and you could tell when you got close that it could be unlatched and slid across, so that whole part of the house could be open to the elements. It was spectacular. So was the way we had placed the burned piece of timber on our knees and what we could now see approaching us from the interior of the house.

It was a man, heavy-set, blond, dishevelled hair, wearing a shining gold housecoat, which he had obviously hastily thrown onto himself since it was wide open in the front, displaying a remarkable pair of pajamas with a Mickey Mouse and Donald Duck pattern, the top buttoned right up to the neck.

What wasn't so spectacular was what he had in his hands. It was a gun, a rifle of some sort, and it didn't look like it was for shooting squirrels. Jim Fiat likely had a weak gun-control policy, and this proved it.

He looked our way anxiously from the other side of the window, then focused on us, and seemed to relax a little. He slid the door back carefully and pointed his weapon right at us.

"It's all right, honey!" he called back over his shoulder. "Nothing to worry about. Just a couple of kids. The security people should be here any minute."

Then he turned back to us and stepped out onto the deck.

"Hello," he snarled.

"Hello, Mr. Fiat," I said pleasantly, "nice jammies."

I heard Antonine laugh.

"Hey, don't I know you?"

"Yes, you looked me right in the face earlier today."

"Really?" He glanced over at Antonine. "And where are you from?"

"I'm from here, Jimmy," she said.

"That's no way to speak to your elders."

"You need to respect them first."

"You can be as smart aleck as you want, but you two are deep trouble. I've unlocked the front door. The security people will be here in five minutes, and I will bring the full force of the law down upon you, believe me. I'm a law and order guy." He looked at me again. "Yes, now I remember. You said you were from Toronto, didn't you? Figures. And bringing her along to do your dirty deed, you should be ashamed of yourself."

"Actually," said Antonine, "I brought him along, not the other way around. My family has lived here for twice as long as yours. No, that's not right, ten times as long...maybe more. Do you recognize this?" She looked down at the burned piece of wood on our knees.

Fiat had taken a few steps forward and was looming over us, his gun still pointed our way, ratcheting up the intimidation factor as high as he figured it could go. Over his shoulder, deep in his house, we could see someone coming into the living room and approaching the window.

"I don't see what a piece of—"

"It comes from your house."

He looked down at it. "Where did you get that?"

"My father found it in the water out on the bay thirteen years ago during one of the most incredible sightings of the ghost ship ever experienced in these parts."

The figure in the house sat down on a chair right near the section of the window Fiat had opened.

We could both see the "man of the people" swallow.

"What does that have to do with me?"

"We thought you might like to tell us yourself," I said. "By the way, we went for a little spin out on the bay earlier today, just as the sun was setting. We explored that little island—" I turned around on the sofa and pointed out toward it. "Right there."

Even from where we were, we could all see a little light on the island, the headlight of a motorboat, which was just beginning to make its way back from a visit out there.

"Oh," said Antonine, "that must be Constable Leblanc. You know, Forensic Identification Section of the Bathurst Police Department?"

"Gabby? Why would she be out there?" asked Fiat. He looked worried and stared out over the water. Then his face relaxed. "I'm pretty sure her parents have one of our lawn signs."

"We found the remains of a body on that island, Jim," I said, "in a shallow grave. Do you know anything about that?"

He appeared not to know what to say.

"My father saw her thrashing around in the water in the vicinity, thirteen years ago, just before he fished out this piece of wood. I saw her, too. She was on fire!"

Jim Fiat looked back and forth from Antonine to me, as if gauging what we knew. Then his face grew red.

"You two think you're really smart, don't you? Coming here and trying to frame me for the death of some immigrant girl. Is someone paying you to do this?"

"Immigrant girl?" asked Antonine.

"Gabrielle Leblanc is a friend of mine, and so is Gaetan Boudreau, the police chief. Gates understands who I am and who I'm about to be. He wouldn't ever consider connecting anything like this to me. He knows how things work."

I could see the figure sitting on the chair in the living room, just on the other side of the window, shuffle uneasily.

"Constable Leblanc has seen the remains by now, Jimmy," said Antonine. "What did you mean by 'immigrant girl?'"

"I don't care whether she's seen the remains or not!" shouted Fiat. "What does that have to do with me?" His last word echoed out over the bay. "A corpse from long ago, some person of no consequence, likely not even identifiable. What does that have to do with me? How does that connect to ME?"

"We have this piece of—" I began.

"So what? Do you think that is the only piece of this sort of wood in the world? And even if it does come from my house, that doesn't mean I had anything to do with it!"

"To do with what?" I said.

"This!" He motioned the gun with a jerk toward the island. Mickey Mouse and Donald Duck jumped up and down.

"Did you?" asked Antonine.

We saw a gleam in his eye.

"Do you know how far I've come to get where I am today? Do you know how other kids made me feel in school around here, just because I was the son of one of the richest people on the beach? The son of the real estate tycoon of the entire region? Do you know what it was like to be nearly failing at school that last year?" He stopped suddenly, as if he had said too much.

"Thirteen years ago?" I asked. We needed him to say more.

He paused. "I wasn't accepted by a single university, not a single one. And Dad, Mr. Christopher Fiat, to whom I was supposed to be a scion, his successor, had planned for me to go to the University of Toronto, or McGill or UBC, some place like that, ride onto one of those campuses on a white horse with a huge scholarship in my hand!" For a second, he almost looked like he was going to tear up.

"I'm an only child, too," I said.

"So am I," said Antonine.

"Yeah, but it was different for you. My father was up for re-election that year. He was looking at three consecutive terms! He hadn't been given a cabinet appointment, nothing, the elites in Ottawa had passed him over time and time again."

"Maybe he didn't deserve it," I suggested.

Fiat glared at me. "How would *you* know? They were sabotaging him from above! That's why the campaign wasn't going well. It looked like he was going to lose. Right when he was building this bloody mansion too, to live here forever like a god of Chaleur Bay. He was in a foul mood just as my rejection notices were coming back from the universities. My failures made him even angrier because he had given me some responsibilities in connection with building the house. He felt like I had let him down." Fiat paused again. "My father hated me...for that. He thought I was useless. He figured I would never make anything of myself."

"What did you do?" asked Antonine. "You did something about it, didn't you?"

"Shut up!" said Jim Fiat. "I don't know why I'm telling you any of this. The security people will be here in another minute or two. In fact, I would have thought they would be here by now. They are likely local people. They won't believe a word you say, burned plank or not. They wouldn't believe I was ever desperate either. Neither would Gabrielle Leblanc and Gates Boudreau. You two are deep trouble. Let's see, once I'm done with you, if you even get to go back to Toronto. I'm sure there's a juvenile hall not far from here just perfect for you."

"Um..." said Antonine, "I'm from here. I've told you that."

Fiat ignored her. "You two think you are better than me, don't you?"

"No," I said.

He paused again. Then he smiled. "Here's what I'm going to do." He looked down, thinking, then back up at us. "I'm going to tell you exactly what happened.

I've let some things out of the bag anyway." He leaned toward us. "Once I've told you my secret, then you will have to live with the fact that you know all this and can do nothing about it. Nothing! No one will accept your story over mine. Not a snowball's chance in hell." He smiled again, though this time with a crazy sort of grin. "I have to get this off my chest anyway," he said quietly, as if to himself.

He stepped back a stride or two and set the gun down so it was resting against his thigh. The shadowy figure in the living room leaned forward.

"It's all understandable, really. I had failed. I had no way of proving myself to my father. The job on the house was a nothing job, something he had given me, and no one could have screwed it up. I was at my wits' end. I didn't have marks in school or Dad's ability in the real estate business or an articulate way of speaking or any real popularity at school. I didn't even have a girlfriend." He glanced toward the house for a second. Then he looked back at us. "I had to do something spectacular!"

"What?" I said. It was almost the id thing. It just came out of me.

"I thought of the ghost ship."

I could hear Antonine gasp.

"I decided to recreate it." Fiat looked over our heads and out across the water as if he were in a trance. "I fudged some purchase invoices and stole some timber from the contractor here and put together a crude raft with a few poles and canvases sticking up so that it might look like a ship from a distance. Then…I needed a girl."

I could feel an actual shiver go down my spine, and the sofa shook a little right beside me.

"I knew many legends about the ship involved a girl," continued Fiat, "wronged somehow, who was at the bow of the vessel, engulfed in flames like the rest of it, haunting the waters of Chaleur Bay." Fiat's eyes looked glazed over. "I told you I didn't have a girlfriend, but it was more than that. I didn't really know any girls or feel comfortable around them, and any girl in her right mind wouldn't want to be part of this sort of thing, anyway, so I was stuck. That was when I encountered her."

"Her?" asked Antonine.

"The girl."

"You don't remember her name?"

"It started with an M. It was short. I think it had two syllables."

"You're a monster," said Antonine quietly.

"Do you want to hear this or not?" asked Fiat.

"Go on," I said, taking Antonine's hand, since she

had seemed like she wanted to get up and leave. "Not yet," I whispered to her.

Fiat wasn't listening, his mind cast back in time again, thirteen years ago.

"I met her downtown at the unemployment office...a place I'd been trying to avoid for a number of weeks, where my father said I had to go to look at job postings for the area. There she was: an immigrant, desperate for a job, looking for menial work, just like Christopher Fiat's son."

I could feel my phone vibrate in my pocket...the phone I'd poached out of Mom and Dad's room while they were sleeping. I pulled it out and slid my thumb across the screen. "MAYA KHAN, AGE 17, LOOKS YOUNGER, DISAPPEARED BATHURST AREA, SEPTEMBER 13 THAT YEAR." I peered over Fiat's shoulder at the figure in the living room.

"Are you looking at your phone?" said Fiat. He shook his head. "Bloody millennial."

"I may not actually qualify as—"

Fiat ignored me. He was in full story mode.

"She was desperate for money. I convinced her to be the young maiden in the boat. She would have done anything for a few dollars...immigrants will. I built my dressed-up raft and paid my little maiden some change to sail on it. We towed it out to a spot on the other side of the island and she got on it, I tied her on, waited for dark, and set it on fire and pushed it off from my boat toward a spot where it could be seen from shore."

My phone vibrated again. I glanced down. "EVERYONE IN MAYA'S FAMILY BUT HER MOTHER KILLED IN A BOMB BLAST IN AFGHANISTAN."

"It was a perfect day to see the ghost ship of legend!" said Fiat. "It was also a day, an early evening, when there were lots of people on the beaches. It felt so good...so good...to make them look at what I had done. Jim Fiat, loser-son of the greatest man in the region. I intended to photograph it. No one, no one in history, had ever done that with any success. No one had ever been close enough for any details to be evident. I would have a ringside seat out there in the bay, with an extraordinary view of the famous ghost ship! I would be able to sell that photograph for a great deal of money, gain acclaim as the only person who ever accomplished the feat, the man who finally proved the existence of the burning ghost ship of Chaleur Bay! James Fiat, me...I would go down in history and profit too. My photograph, which would have been shown on media around the world, would have drawn attention to the region, increased real estate values...I was imagining what my father would think of me then!"

He didn't notice me peek at my phone again. "SHE AND HER MOTHER STRUGGLED IN CANADA."

"It does feel good to get this off my chest. I have told no one. I couldn't."

"MAYA'S MOTHER DIED. MAYA WAS ON HER OWN. NO ONE REPORTED HER MISSING FOR A YEAR."

"The fire, however, took off," said Jim, "the wood was particularly combustible...it was an inferno in minutes. My plan went up in flames."

"And so did she," muttered Antonine.

"I had tied the girl loosely to what I hoped would look like a mast from a distance, just a pole and canvas, really. In her terror, she had a difficult time getting away, and got caught up in the rope...and engulfed in the flames as the ship went under. I remember she screamed."

Antonine put her hands over her face.

"She screamed...and she flailed her way to the island...but died as I raced toward her in my boat. She... she breathed her last gasp just as I got there, expiring at my feet."

Antonine wiped a tear from her eye.

Fiat was staring into the distance. "I buried her in that shallow grave."

The figure in the living room got to its feet.

Fiat shook his head. "I knew something of her situation. I figured she would not be missed, and went on with my life. I am not proud of it, but accidents happen and she was a willing participant. Likely in this country illegally to boot. I...I only had time to take a single terrible photograph and destroyed it soon after." He looked sad. "I had been paralyzed with fear the instant the fire grew out of control. For a short while, I simply watched it burn...listening to her shriek."

The figure from the living room stepped silently out onto the deck behind Fiat.

"Six months later, my father got me into a university, I began working for the family company, did well, knew the art of the deal, and as you know, decided to run for federal office this very year. I have worked my tail off."

I imagined Antonine and Jackson Clay on the other side of the raft from Jim Fiat, getting close to the fire, glimpsing the girl but having to retreat, and Fiat zooming up to the scene as they returned to shore.

"My method and my message to the people of this region burns with truth! No immigrant's indiscretion, no one who tempted me into a mistake, will put a stain on my life! Here is one thing I will guarantee you: I will be more successful than my father—much more!"

The man behind Fiat was wearing a uniform. Bathurst Police Force. He was putting his cellphone—full access to police records —into his pocket.

"I somehow doubt that, Jim," he said.

Fiat whirled around.

"Hello, Chief Boudreau," said Antonine.

"Hello, Mademoiselle Clay. How is your mother?"

"How long have you been here?" demanded Fiat.

"Hell of a story, Jim: that first word being the key one."

We heard the front door creak and Constable Leblanc squeaked and squished toward us, her boots obviously a little wet.

"Gabby!" said Jim Fiat.

She gave him a withering look and kept her distance.

"It was a girl," she said to us, "mid- to late-teen, deceased at about the time of the incident."

"James Fiat, you're under arrest," said Gates Boudreau, "for the manslaughter of one Maya Khan."

He took out a pair of handcuffs and slapped them onto the man of the people.

19

THE INVISIBLE

We were supposed to have been gone by early that morning, but when Mom and Dad came into my room at about 6 A.M. and found me sitting up in my bed with all my clothes on, totally wired, the schedule changed immediately. I told them everything—from finding the burned plank in the Clays' shed, to discovering the remains on the island, to the deal we made with Constable Leblanc and Chief Boudreau, to our daring break-in at Jim Fiat's place...and what the "man of the people" had done long ago. They must have looked at me with their mouths open for about a minute after I was done. Then they told me that I needed to get into bed and go to sleep.

Our departure would be delayed for twenty-four hours. One day. That was going to be all I had left.

Antonine seemed relieved when I called and told her I would be around a little longer. That only made me feel slightly better. It was great that she felt that way, but the clock was ticking. Would she become simply another Wynona Dixon or Dorothy Osborne, lost to me, far away in my past? Or even worse…Alice?

We had to find something to do with the rest of that day, maybe the rest of our lives together. Dad had said we had to be on our way by very early the next morning, even earlier than we'd planned to leave today.

"We will be off at the crack of dawn!" he declared.

Mom took me over to the Clays' house. These last hours were going to be bittersweet. The first part was definitely of the sweet variety. Eve put on another spread of food; I guess her version of a "late lunch." No quinoa, though, thankfully. I tried not to look at the clock ticking on the wall behind Antonine's glorious black hair as I ate, attempting to concentrate on the amazing food instead of us parting. Not only were we going to be in different parts of Canada, but very soon Antonine would be out of the country entirely, entering a new world and making new friends, her life changed forever. I would just be a distant memory, if that.

After we ate, I called Mom on the Clays' landline and asked if I could stay for the rest of the day. Though at the beginning of this trip she would have been opposed to this, arguing that I needed to be a good visitor and spend time, especially these last few hours, with our hosts, she didn't put up a fight of any sort. That might have had something to do with saving Bill from the embarrassment of having to hang out with the kid who told him from the beginning that Jim Fiat was a piece of seagull poop.

"Take your time, honey," said Mom, "but don't propose to her without telling us first."

I hung up the second she said that.

It was a strange experience spending that time at the Clays' house. During a typical day at home in the old days, I would have had my phone going overtime, sorting through other people's lives, celebrities or not, texting Terry and Jason and Rhett. Of course, now I don't even contact them at all. Then I would have fired up Mom and Dad's big HD TV, guiding myself through a little heroic action in some near-reality world in a video game. Maybe I'd be at the head of an evil clan in medieval days, war club in hand, or destroying the rest of the league as I led the Leafs to the cup on the screen.

It was very different with Antonine Marie Clay, goddess of Chaleur Bay. I had almost forgotten that she didn't have a cellphone. That was strange enough, but she didn't own a single video game...or any way to play them on TV. Their television was a little box that looked like it was made in the days before they invented the wheel, and about as thin as a sumo wrestler.

So we just hung out. We talked, we played board games...and it was amazing. Although, I must admit, most of the amazing part was the company.

She was so much fun to be around. She was just so smart and interesting and, well, not too hard to look at...I guess I've said that before, but I have to say it again if I'm telling the truth. After the board games, we went outside and actually played tag, something I thought kids—kids younger than us—played about a million years ago. At times, we laughed so hard we couldn't stay on our feet and just rolled around on the lawn as if we were having fits.

When it came time for dinner, or supper, as Mrs. Clay put it, Antonine said we should take it with us to the beach, just the two of us.

"The Last Supper," said Eve, which I thought was a little dark.

Before we left, Antonine did something funny. She went out to her father's shed and got the burned board. We put it into Eve's little car and took it with us, along with the massive hamper of killer food, and Antonine's bike—she was going to cycle home—and headed for Youghall Beach.

We didn't do a lot on the beach, mostly we just walked. It felt like we went all the way up and down the shore, from Youghall north past the Fiat's massive home, past a place where we had to wade across a bit of water and all the way to a spot called Beresford Beach, and back. We ate half way along the trip. I am likely wrong about us having travelled most of the way up and down the entire beach, because I have the feeling that this killer shoreline of sand in this absolutely beautiful part of the world went a long, long way along the giant bay. We likely could have walked for days.

We talked nearly every second about our lives, about our past, our future. I even told her about Wyn and Dorothy, and believe it or not, Alice. She kind of giggled about all of that. We wondered what it would be like if we ended up knowing each other our whole lives, if when we were old, it would be just like it is right now between us, if we would still like each other or get sick of being together. She talked about how scared she was about the future and living in France, but how excited she was too.

"What do you think was really out there, Antonine?" I asked, "When we chased after that fire? We know now that what you and your dad saw was a burning raft, but what about us, what did we see? Twice! I keep wondering about the vision I had, right in front of me, after you hit your head. It was so vivid."

"I don't know, Dylan. I guess what we saw from land had to be some sort of natural thing that makes fire appear on this water. I guess experts just can't explain it yet. When we got out there, you were pretty wound up; your head had taken that blow too. You likely imagined it.... Who knows, though, maybe Florence is right. Maybe there is something in between."

We smiled at the same time. It felt like nobody else in the world could say that to someone else and totally understand what the other one meant...nobody but us and Florence Green.

By the time we got back to the Youghall area, it was dark. In fact, it had been dark for a long time. We had passed by Bill and Bonnie's place about half an hour before and I had noticed not all the lights were still on in the house. I was late, and by the time we reached

Youghall, it was very late. I wondered if it were past midnight. No phone, couldn't check.

We had hidden Antonine's father's burned board under some bushes at the beach. I wondered why in the world she had wanted to bring it along, but figured it was probably because it was so meaningful to her, to her father, and to us. I thought she just wanted it nearby. Then, she surprised me.

"I want to burn the board," she said.

"Pardon me?"

She pulled some matches out of her jeans. She had brought a sweater along. It was getting colder now. It was a red one and warm looking. She had wrapped it around her hips, now she put it on and it just looked so comfortable on her.

"I want to burn this board and send the smoke into the air. I want it to vanish, forever."

"Vanish? Antonine, this is something that connects you to your father. You want to destroy it?"

"I didn't say that. But I want it to be gone. My father isn't this board. He is in here." She pointed to her heart again. "Remember what I said about invisible things? I don't want him to come back. He can't. I want his spirit though, his invisible, magical spirit, inside me forever."

I thought of Bomb. Then I realized, as we put the board down, set it on fire, and watched the smoke furl into the sky, that what we were doing made me think of Antonine Clay too. She was about to disappear.

Then she kissed me. Very quickly. It seemed over before it began, unfortunately.

"Believe in me," she said.

She squeezed my hand and walked away. I turned and watched her, without saying anything in return. She retrieved her bike from under another bush, flicked on its little light, got on and peddled away without even looking back. I just stood there and watched her. In a few minutes, there was no sign of her and all around me there was absolute silence.

I walked out to the beach and headed back to Bill and Bonnie's place. Before I went inside, I looked out over the water. In the distance, I thought I saw a ball of fire, but when I squinted, I realized that there was nothing there. And yet, the most marvellous feeling filled my heart.

It made me smile.

WE INDEED LEFT AT the crack of dawn the next morning. The parental units actually made a few snide comments about the Bill and Bonnie Show on the way out of town.

It was hilarious. Dad was at the wheel, explaining the history of every place we passed and letting us know the exact population of every town. Mom was making fun of me whenever she got a chance. She seemed very happy, especially when she looked at me—I guess I didn't have that normal sour expression on my mug.

We just zoomed back across the eastern part of our amazing country, through New Brunswick and Quebec, back home to Toronto. Bomber didn't make a single appearance in the back seat with me, but that didn't mean he wasn't there. He was in my heart. Dylan Maples's heart.

I was thinking about Rhett, Jason, and Terry too, and about a couple of people in my class with whom I figured I might hang out. I had Antonine's invisible necklace on, tucked under my T-shirt. I liked the fact that no one could see it and not because I was ashamed of it.

"Can I have my phone, Mom?"

She looked at Dad.

"Why?" she asked.

"I have to text a friend." I paused. "No, I have to call him." Then I paused again. "Three of them, actually."